WORLDS OF WONDER

Edited By Lynsey Evans

First published in Great Britain in 2024 by:

Young Writers
Remus House
Coltsfoot Drive
Peterborough
PE2 9BF
Telephone: 01733 890066
Website: www.youngwriters.co.uk

All Rights Reserved
Book Design by Ashley Janson
© Copyright Contributors 2024
Softback ISBN 978-1-83565-243-5

Printed and bound in the UK by BookPrintingUK
Website: www.bookprintinguk.com
YB0582M

FOREWORD

Welcome Reader!

Are you ready to discover weird and wonderful creatures that you'd never even dreamed of?

For Young Writers' latest competition we asked primary school pupils to create a creature of their own invention, and then write a story about it using just 100 words - a hard task! However, they rose to the challenge magnificently and the result is this fantastic collection full of creepy critters and bizarre beasts!

Here at Young Writers our aim is to encourage creativity in children and to inspire a love of the written word, so it's great to get such an amazing response, with some absolutely fantastic stories.

Not only have these young authors created imaginative and inventive creatures, they've also crafted wonderful tales to showcase their creations. These stories are brimming with inspiration and cover a wide range of themes and emotions - from fun to fear and back again!

I'd like to congratulate all the young authors in this anthology, I hope this inspires them to continue with their creative writing.

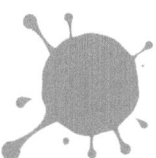

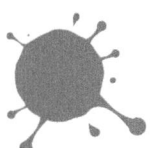

CONTENTS

Cransley School, Great Budworth

Seb Holme (10)	1
Ben Hughes (11)	2
Emmy Tomlisson (10)	3
Sasha Elizabeth Bryan (10)	4
Orla Kay (11)	5
Malilda Rees (10)	6
Samuel Baggott (10)	7
Ethan Loom (10)	8
Maximus Knowles (11)	9
Michael O'Neill (10)	10
Isaac Campbell (10)	11
Lauren Cunnah (10)	12
Huxley Tottle (10)	13
Xander West (11)	14
Isabella Batchelor (11)	15
Sebastian Buckingham (11)	16
Barney Welch (10)	17
Ava Watterson (10)	18
Oliver Colling (10)	19
Sebastian Orange (10)	20
Joseph Albinson (11)	21

Downside Primary School, Luton

Aisha Azad (11)	22
Mishaal Farooq (10)	23
Fatima Iman (11)	24
Daria-Aliseia Gaidos (10)	25
Parsa Ahmed (10)	26
Rebecca Gurung (10)	27

Fairley House Junior School, London

Arthur Ayles (9)	28
Josephine Eussen (10)	29
Eleanor Eussen (9)	30
Noah Saul (9)	31
Rosa Marsh (10)	32
Petra Cantaouzene-Speransky (9)	33
Nadia Atassi (8)	34
Aisha Ronte (8)	35

Hart Memorial Primary School, Portadown

Eilidh Lyness (10)	36
Annalise McLoughlin (9)	37
Foyez Rahman (10)	38
Andre Abreu (10)	39
Rosie Forde (9)	40
Sophie Ifteni (10)	41
Borislava Nikolova (10)	42
Christopher Lappin (9)	43
Robyn Ficetola (9)	44
Elyssia Lewis (10)	45
Rebecca Smyth (9)	46
Lucas Patton (10)	47
Noah Grant (10)	48
Bobby Scott (9)	49
Nikola Nogaj (9)	50
Anika Briede (10)	51
Lukas Kaskonas (10)	52
Taylon Carvalho (10)	53
Cole Mcandless (10)	54
Emily Magee (9)	55
Ellie-Mae (9)	56

Owen Gardiner (9)	57
Mia-Louise Craven (9)	58
Jayden Watson (9)	59
Jaxon Armstrong (10)	60
Sophie Goncalves (10)	61
Joao Molinet (10)	62
Nadia Harhari (9)	63
Lukas Baranovskis (9)	64
Sally Steinberg (10)	65
Bobby Woods (10)	66
Ella McCann (10)	67
Kajus Penkauskas (10)	68
Cristovao Azinhais (10)	69
Tyler Maguire (9)	70
Danny Crawford (9)	71
Macey Oliver (9)	72
Lucy Roycroft (10)	73
Wojciech Jarosz (9)	74
Caleb Dawson (10)	75
Jensen Orr (9)	76

Lakefield CofE Primary School, Gloucester

George Alperwick (9)	77
Lula-Rose Lusty (10)	78
Sonny Reid (9)	79
Connie Fouracres (9)	80
Alice Currie (9)	81
Ava Jackson (9)	82
Winnie Price (9)	83
George Price (9)	84
Erin O'Gorman-Jevons (9)	85
William Cabb (9)	86
Ruby Turner (9)	87
Clementine Shayle (9)	88
Daniel Widgery (9)	89
Esme Peacey (10)	90
Poppy Ramsdale (9)	91
Harry Knight (9)	92
Ben Oliveri (10)	93
Olivia Burrus (9)	94
Niamh Rodway (9)	95
Chloe Price (10)	96
Zac George (10)	97

New Horizons Primary School, Portsmouth

Winnie Glossop (8)	98
Dara Sonubi (9)	99
EwaogoOluwa Adefioye (9)	100
Megan Browning (10)	101
Maddie-May Nash (9)	102
Phoebe Neary (9)	103
Harrison Winmill (8)	104
Lucy Holden (9)	105
Tomasz Wygowski (9)	106
Anya Mitchell (9)	107
Patrik Dascalescu (9)	108

Springwell Park Community Primary School, Bootle

James Hemmings (9)	109
Erika Domnitanu (9)	110
Ella Rowley (9)	111
Vanessa Wezyk (9)	112
Charlie Jones (10)	113

St Agnes' Catholic Primary School, Crawcrook

William Madl (8)	114
Neve Ball (8)	115
Thomas Rafferty (8)	116
Isabelle Batsford (8)	117
Clara Cantrill (9)	118
Phoebe Catterall (9)	119
Ethan Richardson (8)	120
Imogen Rodgers (8)	121
Theo Sage (8)	122
Jessica Slegg (8)	123
Annabelle Slegg (8)	124
Isaac Beading (8)	125
Isaac Mason Burnett (8)	126
Mia Blake (8)	127
Emily Williams (8)	128

Ed Johnson (8)	129
Thea Exley (8)	130
Ella Williams (8)	131
Phoebe Stephenson (9)	132
Reuben Roberts (9)	133
Kristian Hutchinson (8)	134
Finlay Curry (8)	135
Emile Goss (9)	136

St Mark's CofE Primary School, Stoke-On-Trent

Zainab Qayum (10)	137
Fatimah Zaheer (10)	138
Ana-Maria Mitran (10)	139
Mason Paul Buxton (10)	140

St Mary's School, Gerrards Cross

Jaslena Manka (8)	141
Jahnavi Misra (11)	142
Ishani Dhamecha (10)	143
Jayna Master (8)	144
Jaya Bass (10)	145
Katie Donaghey (8)	146

St Michael's CE (VC) Junior School, Twerton

Freya Hill (11)	147
Jessica Rose Hill (10)	148

St Robert Bellarmine Catholic Primary School, Bootle

Autumn Reardon (7)	149
Emily Powell (7)	150
Scarlett Green (7)	151
Dylan Hurley (8)	152
Jasmine Wilson (8)	153
Archie Owens (7)	154

St Silas CE Primary School, Blackburn

Anaya Taher (10)	155
Daniyal Ahmed (9)	156
Fatima Patel (9)	157
Haadiya Saifullah (9)	158
Aliya Nisar (10)	159
Affan Usman (10)	160
Daniyal Miah (9)	161
Rayhaan Garner (9)	162
Arifah Begum (9)	163
Layla Shifa (9)	164
Rebin Taher (9)	165
Mohammed Khalid (9)	166
Rayyan Bhayat (9)	167
Sabir Hussain (9)	168
Albina Nesenenko (9)	169
Ibrahim Sher (9)	170
Denis Sercaianu (10)	171

St Thomas' Primary School, Riddrie

Fearne Dawson (8)	172
Myla Donaldson (8)	173
Dempsey Patterson (8)	174
Charlie Harrigan (8)	175
Chimamanda Nwankwo (8)	176
Elyse Bennett (8)	177
Uzochi Egbunefu (8)	178
Thomas Docherty (7)	179
Chloe Kawalec (7)	180
Georgia McConnell (7)	181
Nathan Bremner (8)	182
Sean-Patrick Miller (8)	183
Grace Fitzpatrick (8)	184
Emmanuel O'Poku (8)	185

THE STORIES

The Monster Who Didn't Tidy His Room

Little Monster was outside having a nice day playing with his monster friends in the woods until his mum shouted, "Come here now and tidy your room."
"No," Little Monster shouted.
"Come here now!" his mum shouted more seriously than last time.
"I said no," Little Monster shouted even louder.
"You will lose your screen time," Mum said.
"Fine," Little Monster said.
So Little Monster went back to the house and tidied his room and then went back to playing for about another hour or two and still got screen time. He'd tidied his room so everyone was happy.

Seb Holme (10)
Cransley School, Great Budworth

Mechanical Dragon War Human

One human, the only human left in existence after the quantum destruction of humans, was transported to Dragotaurus's home of mechanical minigonclops and the dragfins. The mechanical minigonclops adopted the last human child called Doomsday Man. The minigonclops taught the human the dragclop ways, including roaring and eating loads of food. One day, the human was sent to war against the Dragfins with the mechanical dragon laser beam to kill all in its sight and take no prisoners. Three years later, the human destroyed the entire planet to stop this war, leaving barely any survivors, but then...

Ben Hughes (11)
Cransley School, Great Budworth

Ceven's Crazy Day!

It was a normal Wednesday. Ceven was on his way to work when something out of the ordinary happened.
Suddenly, he felt a shiver racing up his spine; it felt like he was paralysed with fear.
Whilst his body was still, he felt his feet beginning to hover over the ground. That's when he was suddenly sucked up into a colossal spaceship high above the clouds.
Ceven looked around and found himself surrounded by humans. Real-life humans!
He had only ever seen humans in a storybook.
If they're as bad as they are in stories, "Aggghh! Help!" thought Ceven.

Emmy Tomlisson (10)
Cransley School, Great Budworth

An Alien Called Brainy

At school, Amber started to act really naughty, but could not stop herself.
"Miss, you've got a hairy chin!" she shouted whilst throwing balls of paper at her classmates. Next, she knocked everyone's work on the floor. She felt her mind was being controlled. From her blazer pocket, a little worm-like creature appeared. It looked up at Amber without speaking and told her it had control of her mind and had teleported into her pocket by mistake. It was bored, so it decided to create mischief. As fast as he arrived he left, leaving Amber in shock but with detention.

Sasha Elizabeth Bryan (10)
Cransley School, Great Budworth

The Scare Of The Snapped At Creature

One dark, gloomy, foggy morning there was a sad, depressed, angry and snappy creature who really looked very snake-like. He had red, scaly skin and a very dense unibrow with brown eyes. All day, every day, he spent his hours snapping at everyone he passed by. One lunchtime, Snappy even went up to somebody and said, "Give me three pieces of your cake or I'll tell every creature in this forest you still wear nappies!"

Everybody really hated Snappy, so they decided they needed revenge. They put nine snails under Snappy's pillow at night. The next day he felt bad.

Orla Kay (11)
Cransley School, Great Budworth

The Little Monster Who Changes Feeling

In a land named Earth lived a very unique soul called Cupcake. She had a young, fluffy body. She was only small, but her determination was definitely the opposite. Cupcake was fluttering about something that caught her eye. It was someone being cruel to a little girl. Cupcake couldn't stand this! She watched in awe as the little girl sobbed her poor eyes out. Cupcake was desperate to help but knew she was only a little monster. This wasn't getting past her. She found the courage and showed the bully who was boss because in her heart, meanness isn't tolerated!

Malilda Rees (10)
Cransley School, Great Budworth

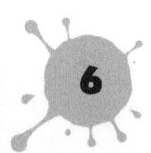

Dooey

As the school pupils walked into school, expecting a normal day, Miss Erable, the school teacher, introduced a new student called Dooey. He wasn't an ordinary student because Dooey was from Neptune. Neptune was the centre of the universe for joke teasing. Dooey was on a special mission to make everyone laugh. He was armed with his funniest joke because he knew how important it was to laugh. His joke was: "Where do you learn to make ice cream? Sundae School." This made everyone laugh loudly, and Miss Erable decided to change her name to Miss Happy with a Flake.

Samuel Baggott (10)
Cransley School, Great Budworth

Helpful Goofini Wood

Goofini Wood looked at the squishy map in his hands and felt war. He walked over to the window and reflected on his grand surroundings. He had always loved picturesque Planet Flash, until one day the sides of the planet got into an argument about which side was better. This eventually led to war with hundreds of aliens dying. The leader of the other side was called Renegade. She had long brunette legs and despised Goofini. A few years had passed and Goofini and Renegade met to have a discussion about the war. Goofini told Renegade, "I am your father."

Ethan Loom (10)
Cransley School, Great Budworth

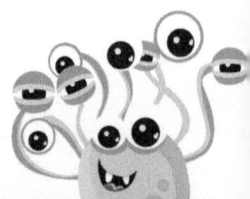

The Eat Everything Blob

Once upon a time, there was an old abandoned mine where a mushroom was forming. Suddenly, slime started to spew out of the mushroom, forming a car-sized blob! The first thing the blob did was devour the mushroom it came from because the only way a blob could be stopped was by its mushroom. Travelling at its top speed of 15mph, the blob headed to the city, eating everything in its way. It'd now consumed 1,000 million calories. It reached the city, consuming whole buildings. The blob was disappointed because the people tasted worse than cows, what a let down!

Maximus Knowles (11)
Cransley School, Great Budworth

The Friendly Monster

Jamal was in school. He never liked school. There was never anything exciting going on. Then one day, there was something he found interesting: a weird voice from the bushes. It was distorted. Then suddenly, an alien-like creature came out. Jamal sprinted, scared for his life. The next day, he went back to the same spot to see the monster. This time, not fearful for his life, he started talking to him even though he had five eyes and was stinky! One day, he disappeared. Behind him Jamal heard a scarier voice, very different from his friend's, but then...

Michael O'Neill (10)
Cransley School, Great Budworth

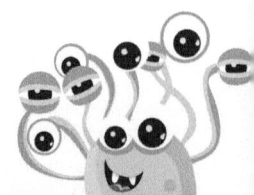

The Spooky Spider

Tap, tap, tap. You turn around and see the most enormous spider to ever exist! Its massive, claw-like legs start thudding towards you, gradually getting closer with each step until it finally reaches you. It lets out a chilling shriek, showing you its massive jaws. You want to run, but you can't move. You want to scream, but you can't make a noise. Suddenly, the gargantuan arachnid takes one final stride, venomous saliva oozing from its gigantic mouth, and you run like you have never run before, the spider trailing close behind you...

Isaac Campbell (10)
Cransley School, Great Budworth

The Creature From Openopele

The sun beamed over the water as Bob swam around. Other strange creatures roamed the lush fields of Openopele. Suddenly, out of nowhere, a gargantuan spaceship came down and started searching for the perfect creature to take back to their lab to experiment on. Bob was unaware of the situation, deciding to warm up in the sun, but it was too late. Back at the lab, the humans decided to experiment on Bob, unaware of his hidden strength: his tongue. Bob speedily whisked himself back to Openopele with his tongue! It's strange but true!

Lauren Cunnah (10)
Cransley School, Great Budworth

The Takeover

There once was a man called Borgan who died. Sadly, he was run over to death. Then, a year later, he woke up as a skeleton. He set off to his home, and everyone screamed in terror as he came by. Then he looked at his hands and jumped; he was a skeleton. Borgan was intrigued by this discovery, and he started scaring people around his village. Next time, people started to not be scared. So, he started scaring people in other towns and villages until everyone wasn't scared of him. People started getting angry at him, so he died.

Huxley Tottle (10)
Cransley School, Great Budworth

Tsew's Adventure

On a planet far, far away lived a little monster called Tsew Rednax. He was hairy, red and had three piercing blue eyes that could look in several directions at the same time. One day, he decided to go on an adventure and heard amazing stories about a planet called Earth and a sport that he had never heard of before that sounded fun and interesting, which humans liked to play, called football. So, he packed his space ball and set off in his rocket, excited to discover the new surroundings and what life is like on Earth.

Xander West (11)
Cransley School, Great Budworth

Zuto's Lucky Day

One day, Zuto started a new school. He was very nervous and didn't think he was going to make any friends.

As soon as he walked through the school doors, people laughed at him. He cried and ran to the bathroom. After an entire week of people laughing at him, he wished he had stayed at his old school. That was until one day when a little boy walked in. Everyone laughed at him too.

The new alien told everyone to stop, as it was very mean. Zuto ran up to him.

"How do you do it?" They hugged.

Isabella Batchelor (11)
Cransley School, Great Budworth

The Adventure Of Jeff And Jewy

One day, a boy named Jeff randomly got teleported to a different universe, and he was jelly! He was in Jelly World. Everyone was jelly, a blob of jelly. He couldn't believe his eyes! At first, he thought it was all a dream but soon realised it wasn't a dream. The next day, he met another jelly, and his name was Jewy. A week later, they were best friends but soon found out there was another one of them but red and they were evil, so they defeated them in a battle! They went on to rule the universe!

Sebastian Buckingham (11)
Cransley School, Great Budworth

Harry The Hog

Harry, the happy Hog, lives on Planet Hog. After finishing his shopping for grass burgers and grass shakes, Harry started to stroll home along the hog path from the Super Hog-market. Harry spotted a crime against grass. Bad hogs were stealing a family pack of grass burgers from an innocent family of hogs! Harry caught them hog-handed and, as quick as a flash, oinked them into oblivion - crime cracked, hog style! After Harry's hog-tastic day, he celebrated with Hog-Donald's and a bottle of Hog-secco.

Barney Welch (10)
Cransley School, Great Budworth

New School

Jasper was a new student at Creature High. He was a little different from everyone else. He was a frog. There weren't a lot of frogs in Creature High so it was hard for him to make friends. Every time he tried to talk to someone they'd make fun of him because of the way he looked. His birthday was coming up. He sent out invites, but on the day of his birthday, no one came. So the next day he went to school all sad and lonely, until Jasper met another frog. They were in shock and became friends.

Ava Watterson (10)
Cransley School, Great Budworth

One Piece

Once there was a pirate, the king of the pirates. He was captured during battle by the Marines. That day he would get beheaded. The guy with the axe asked him, "Any last words?"
The king of the pirates said, "Yes, I hid a treasure chest across the seas, go!"
Everyone rushed out to their pirate ships.
There was one person who ate the special fruit that granted magical powers. The fruit made him turn into rubber.
Luffy screamed, "And on we go!"

Oliver Colling (10)
Cransley School, Great Budworth

The Dreaded Blanks

Jake was sitting in front of his computer screen. You see, Jake had to submit a piece of homework, but he had a case of the blanks. He didn't know it yet, but as he was about to give up, he saw some fruit in the fruit bowl. The blanks are peculiar creatures; they are highly intolerant to fruit. So, he took a bite of his banana, and he let out the loudest burp ever! This is how blanks came out. Then Jake carried on with his homework and finished it! The next day, he had got an A+!

Sebastian Orange (10)
Cransley School, Great Budworth

Master

Once in Alaska, a scientist called Mr McButan once dropped a piece of play dough in a red bed. It started growing and spewing out like a volcano until he was confused by the sludge. It became a part of him.

Joseph Albinson (11)
Cransley School, Great Budworth

Felicity's Journey To Restore Balance

In the enchanted land of Avaloria, Felicity, a three-eyed guardian with the body of a sleek cat protected the magic that flowed through the world. Her rival, the malevolent Shadowfang, targeted her magic.

Guided by intuition, she discovered a portal to an ominous realm where Shadowfang stole magic from an ancient tree. In a fierce battle, Felicity banished the darkness, restoring balance to Avaloria.

Exhausted yet triumphant, she returned to her forest sanctuary, celebrated as the one-eyed guardian. With unwavering resolve, Felicity continued to protect Avaloria's magic, forever remembered as a symbol of courage and protection in the land.

Aisha Azad (11)
Downside Primary School, Luton

Cornell Saves The Day

On Planet Fear, a creature named Fiery sat in his science lesson, bored and restless. The teacher droned on about chemical reactions and formulae that held no interest for Fiery. Just as he was about to unleash his mighty yawn, something magical happened. He transformed into an electric bat, causing all the chemicals to light on fire. Out of nowhere, Cornell, his best friend, had saved him, pulling the fire alarm and using the extinguisher to stop the fire from spreading.
"Evacuate!" bellowed the students as they rushed out of the classroom.

Mishaal Farooq (10)
Downside Primary School, Luton

Snow

I woke up twisting and turning. I took a look at my calendar, then I realised it was a Monday. I shoved my face into my pillow, already wanting the day to end. I'd been lying in my bed peacefully for thirty minutes when the silence was broken.
"Frost! I think you might want to come outside!"
I sat up and let out a groan as my tentacles shivered. Wait, they shivered? Wait, then that means...
I rushed outside filled with excitement. I felt the icy wind course through my tentacles, then I shouted, "It's snowing!"

Fatima Iman (11)
Downside Primary School, Luton

Perfectly Imperfect

Centuries ago, in Ghosteria, Angel was born, but there was something peculiar about her. She had wings but she wasn't able to float like the rest. She read of spells, magic and potions but not a single thing worked. Despite the fact that she had gorgeous, delicate wings that arched behind her in the softest colour of grey, it still wasn't enough. Angel attempted to disguise her wings to keep them a secret from the world.

But why hide away the thing that makes you special and unique from the rest? Let nobody stop you for you are amazing.

Daria-Aliseia Gaidos (10)
Downside Primary School, Luton

Agent Suri Vs Messy Otoki

In a beautiful place called Roseland, a monster named Suri was a secret agent. One day, she received a mission to capture the world's worst monster, Messy Otoki. Agent Suri knew that this was the job for her, so she put on her suit and headed for where Messy Otoki was. Suri found Messy Otoki, and when she wasn't looking, Suri put a net over her, and there was no escape. Agent Suri got an award for capturing Messy Otoki because if she hadn't, Roseland would be a really messy place. Agent Suri was the best agent in the world.

Parsa Ahmed (10)
Downside Primary School, Luton

Karma!

One late night on Nightingale Road, Stormii was going on her evening stroll through the park when Dikui, the neighbour's dog, was also going on a walk. He spotted Stormii and a smirk slowly grew on his face as he crept towards her, placing a paw on her body and making her flinch. After scolding him, she strutted home with a pout on her face. He repeated that every night until one night when he touched her. She didn't flinch but instead released quills at him, causing him to shed tears, roll around and try to pull out the spikes.

Rebecca Gurung (10)
Downside Primary School, Luton

Left Home

An asteroid hits planet Vergeel! Millions of dragon-like beasts emerge from the crumbled asteroid. Quiznak, the five-eyed alien, is the only one who can defeat them. He uses his undestroyable cannon but fails. He feels sad and scared that the army will immobilise and destroy him. Quiznak runs to the escape pod and lands on Planet Earth! Quiznak is a very clever alien and he hears a message from the giant ship - "Earth is next to be destroyed by Destrucdoid..."
Quiznak tells the humans, who listen and pick up every type of weapon, "Defeat Destrucdoid and live together in peace!"

Arthur Ayles (9)
Fairley House Junior School, London

Gruner: The Monster's New Home

"Josephine!" my mum yelled.
"What did I do?"
This has been happening all day. My dirty clothes keep ending up on the floor. I want to blame my brother, Nicklas, but he is not here.
"I have asked you multiple times! Put your dirty clothes *into* the basket."
I trudge to my room again and pick up my clothes. As I do, I see the cause of my never-ending misery. A green ball of fur with chicken legs.
My only chance is to relocate him and I show him to Nick's door.
Then my mum calls, "Nick!"

Josephine Eussen (10)
Fairley House Junior School, London

The Milky Way

Bob Bilius and Cow were fighting over a Milky Way candy bar. Bob said it was his because a friend gave it to him. Cow said it was his because Bob dropped it and Cow found and ate it. Cow used his superpower to turn invisible, but Bob saw his footprints in the ooey-gooey surface of Gooey Planet.
Big Friendly Giant (BFG) saw them fighting and told them to stop.
Bob said, "Cow started it!"
Cow said, "Finders keepers!"
BFG got a new Milky Way and gave it to Bob. Friends don't fight with friends.

Eleanor Eussen (9)
Fairley House Junior School, London

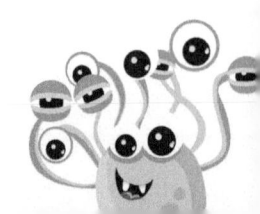

Vadar And Godzilla

Once there were two brothers, Vadar and Godzilla. Vadar and Godzilla split with their family because they hated each other and their family hated each other, so they split up. Half of the family were on Godzilla's side and half on Vadar's side. Five hundred years later, they found each other and went to hell to fight. They fought for a thousand years. That's why people don't believe in monsters, because they're all fighting. One day they lost each other so they started haunting people.

Noah Saul (9)
Fairley House Junior School, London

The Mars Monster

Soos is a monster from Mars. He has wings and his special power is water magic. Before Soos got to Earth it was one big rock. Soos got hungrier than ever so he flew down to Earth and ate two continents. He got full so he cast a spell to rain down water on Earth. That's why we have rivers, streams and seas. He flew back to Mars and he never wanted to go down to Earth again so, when he is hungry, he now goes to the moon to eat. That's why the moon is sometimes not whole.

Rosa Marsh (10)
Fairley House Junior School, London

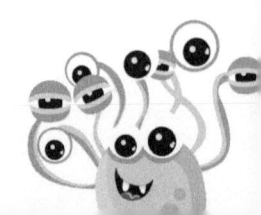

Untitled

It all started with lots of beautiful, amazing, wonderful fairies living in a small, cute cottage in colourful Austria. Sadly and stupidly, they were envied.
The giants bombed the fairies' cottage, so all the beautiful, amazing, wonderful fairies had to go far away. Sadly, they had to split apart. It was very, very sad. The beautiful, amazing, wonderful Lilow went to colourful, but hot, Australia and lived the best, happiest, amazing life there.

Petra Cantaouzene-Speransky (9)
Fairley House Junior School, London

Booba's Earth Adventure

Booba was a crazy creature who lived on Mars. She got bored and decided to travel the universe. She discovered Planet Earth and thought it was beautiful, but she was surprised there was sadness everywhere.
Booba couldn't fix the problem by herself, so she messaged her friends on WhatsApp to come and help. They came in huge spaceships and invaded Earth, but it was worth it because they brought happiness and joy.

Nadia Atassi (8)
Fairley House Junior School, London

Mr Chicken Head

Mr Chicken Head is tall and skinny and he likes farting. His daughter, called House, looks like a colourful croissant. They stole a red car on the way to space and said hello to the planets ahead. They drank their alien smoothies as they went. House has a brother called Water Bottle because he looks like a water bottle. He likes making spectacular gardens out of pasta.

Aisha Ronte (8)
Fairley House Junior School, London

Who Or What Was That?

I was just going for a calm walk.
"Arghhh!" I screamed.
Someone had just grabbed my neck and thrown me on the ground. I picked myself up.
"What was that?"
I ran to my friend's house and told her what happened.
She said, "Come on, let's investigate."
We went into the bushes.
"Arghhh!"
We both went down.
"What was that?" my friend said.
"That's what happened to me."
"Okay, let's look some more."
"Really? After all that?"
"Yes, come on."
We walked through the forest for hours.
"Ewww!"
We found a dead deer with a stick stuck inside it and blood gushing out.

Eilidh Lyness (10)
Hart Memorial Primary School, Portadown

The Christmas Eve Mission

"Santa, who am I the monster-elf of?"
"Ho Ho. You are the monster-elf of Tom and Maddie."
"Alright. See you later tonight, Santa."
"Goodbye, Miles."
"Hi there."
"Oh, hello," said Tom. Tom invited Miles to the house.
When they got in, Maddie said, *"Get out!"* Miles felt it would be a long December, so Miles tried everything he possibly could, but nothing would work, not even their favourite things would work. Eventually, it got to Christmas Eve. Miles was worried that Santa would bring coal. Miles hated it when children didn't get anything.
Did they...?

Annalise McLoughlin (9)
Hart Memorial Primary School, Portadown

Disaster

Once upon a time, there was this kid called Alex. He wasn't a good kid but then one day a meteor came flying from Mars. When it landed, a lot of smoke came out of the meteor. Then a monstrous creature came out. Everyone started to run but Alex stayed. The monster said, "Thank you for staying. An evil scientist tried to kill me."
"I will save you."
"Thanks."
"Let's go fly there."
"Okay. There he is. The scientist."
"Hey you. Take this." He threw a metal pipe at him. He got crushed.
"Let's go back."
"Okay."
"Did he die?"

Foyez Rahman (10)
Hart Memorial Primary School, Portadown

Gooye The Ghost Lands On Earth

Once upon a time, when Gooye the Ghost was flying his spaceship to Mars, Spacer Kari, a good man came and blasted Gooye with a laser. It destroyed Gooye's spaceship and landed on Earth. When he was there, he saw lights, Christmas carols and Christmas trees. Gooye was shocked. He asked people where he was and they said, "Pardon?"
"Where do I get my spaceship fixed?" said Gooye.
She said, "Yes, follow me." He followed her and got led to Santa Claus.
Gooye said to Santa, "Can you fix my spaceship?"
"Yes."
"Thanks." And went to Mars.

Andre Abreu (10)
Hart Memorial Primary School, Portadown

Saving Slime Land

It's a peaceful day in Slime Land. When the alarm rings... *The boot that holds happiness is gone!* I, Slimo, run to the palace. "Slime, can you get the boot!" exclaims the queen.
"Yes."
Next, I get into the spaceship. *Zoom!* I shoot up. Then, I go to Earth. *Snap. Crackle. Pop!* I crash land. "Ugh, it probably floated to around here. I need to find my way home. Ahh, north!" *Whoosh! Boom!* "Oh, my head!"
"Ah, you got it, you got it! Thank you so much. You saved everyone. You're the best," says the queen.

Rosie Forde (9)
Hart Memorial Primary School, Portadown

Shop Storm

Izzy and her friend Gwen were Christmas shopping to get in the Christmas spirit. As they were shopping, they saw a grey shadow in the sky. Everyone gasped and screamed. Izzy and Gwen were confused. "What's happening?" said Izzy. Someone shouted, "The snow monster is coming." I slowly turned around and felt an icy breeze coming towards me. The big, blue snow monster was sprinting towards me. I felt sick to my stomach and looked in my pockets but there was nothing. Suddenly, a flame-thrower magically appeared. I pressed the red button and melted him. Now, Christmas was saved!

Sophie Ifteni (10)
Hart Memorial Primary School, Portadown

The Friendly Creature

Once upon a time, there was a little creature called Moon. Moon was a little creature that was so playful. But one day, he was so sad that one creature said, "Hi, Moon. Are you okay?"
And Moon said, "I lost my lollipop. I am so sad."
And then they searched and searched and they found it. And then the guy who helped him said, "My name is Jake. Nice to meet you. Where do you get the lollipops?"
And Moon said, "Over there, do you see that shop?"
"Okay, I will come with you."
"Okay."
They got the lollipop.

Borislava Nikolova (10)
Hart Memorial Primary School, Portadown

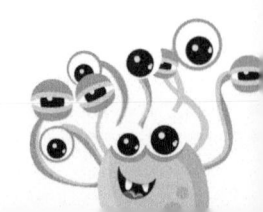

Big Jim Saves The Day!

Christopher was playing football for Rangers in the cup final. In the last few minutes of the match, Rangers were winning 1-0 thanks to Christopher's wonder goal he scored in the first half. Aberdeen were pressing hard for an equaliser. Their star striker, Jeremy, was through on goal when Ranger's goalkeeper came out and took him down. *Penalty!* He was sent off! Big Jim, the reserve goalkeeper, was brought on in place of Christopher. Jeremy struck the ball perfectly. It headed for the goal when Big Jim stretched out his long arms and caught the ball. He'd saved the day!

Christopher Lappin (9)
Hart Memorial Primary School, Portadown

The Battle

Monika was doing a lot of ink tricks when suddenly, water splashed her.

Aqua, thought Monika.

"What's the matter?" teased Aqua.

Monika got so angry that she used all her power to shoot the biggest ink splotch in the world... There was complete silence for a moment. Then water started to dart at her. Monika dodged most of it, but if even a drop of water got on her ink watch, she'd die. Her ink watch kept her alive. But suddenly, water got on her ink watch. Monika started to evaporate. Aqua laughed menacingly. Monika ran away desperately to live...

Robyn Ficetola (9)
Hart Memorial Primary School, Portadown

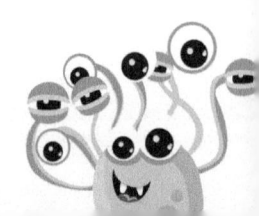

The Most Wiggliest Saga

Wiggles is a round monster that wiggles to great things. His worst enemy is Jiggles, another monstrous creature in the USA. Jiggles and Wiggles are the most monstrous creatures out there. Then one evening, Wiggles was playing at the beach with his ball. Out of nowhere, Jiggles came and stole his ball then said, "Haha." And off he went.

Wiggles chased after him at full sprint. Out of nowhere, Jiggles tripped over a rock. So then the inflatable ball burst. Jiggles ran off.

"What have you done?" Wiggles said.

The ball had a hole in it, forever enemies.

Elyssia Lewis (10)
Hart Memorial Primary School, Portadown

The Dusty Monster

Dusty was watching and waiting for his favourite part of the day... bedtime! Socks would come off, leaving toe fluff for eating. Nobody felt Dusty eating their fluff when they were deeply asleep. That was until the lights went on...
He heard a girl shout. "What happened to my fluff?"
He looked at the clock. "7 o'clock," he said quietly. He jumped into a dirty sock and ate the fluff. The sock moved. He knew he was in danger of being squished. Luckily, a hole in the sock allowed him to escape. Dusty hid, afraid of the sock forever.

Rebecca Smyth (9)
Hart Memorial Primary School, Portadown

Zipper And The Treasure

Zipper goes on a walk to find the treasure. On the path to go to the treasure, Coreva steals the treasure map. Zipper runs after her and grabs the map back. Coreva runs up the steep mountain after Zipper. Coreva tries to snatch the map off Zipper. Zipper starts running faster up the mountain. Coreva not far behind. Zipper sees the treasure far ahead. Zipper's heart beating faster and faster. Coreva starts catching up, not far from Zipper. Now, Zipper grabs the treasure. Then Zipper calls for the lift home in the ship. The ship came. Zipper was safe now.

Lucas Patton (10)
Hart Memorial Primary School, Portadown

The Blob Who Went To Earth

There once was a green blob that really wanted to go to Earth. He lived on Planet Fartsmeller. He had no friends, but really wanted an adventure.
So one day, he decided to actually go to Earth. He was so excited that he started turning yellow. The yellow/green blob got his spacewear on and stepped on the flying ship. He was zooming through the galaxy and finally landed on Earth. He was so excited, but when he got out of the ship, everybody started running and screaming, "There's an alien! Everybody run and hide! Be careful, people!"

Noah Grant (10)
Hart Memorial Primary School, Portadown

The School Breakdown

Divine's eight eyes blinked back tears. Hiding in the janitor's closet, Divine thought about the bullies teasing him for having no parents. Running out of the school, he went to his alley and two random creatures began to chase him. He went to sleep. When he woke, he was in a test tube. He remembered he could bite the glass to escape, so he did. He ran through the laboratory. He saw an exit, but then saw different pictures of him. There was a note. It said: 'I'm sorry, son'. His parents came out and they lived happily ever after.

Bobby Scott (9)
Hart Memorial Primary School, Portadown

Creature From Venus

Loly landed on Earth and started walking around Earth. Then Loly met some people. The people were scared, but later they became friends.
A couple of weeks passed and she had to go back to Venus. She went back home. Loly sighed, "Bye!" The people answered, "Bye-bye!"
She got on her spaceship and flew away through the clouds, through the stars and she finally landed on Venus. Loly told her mum and dad about what she had done and that she had lots of fun. Then she ate a sandwich, got on her bed and fell asleep.

Nikola Nogaj (9)
Hart Memorial Primary School, Portadown

Untitled

Brancil went on a journey to find gems for his necklaces but met seven gremlins along the way. They tried stopping him but unfortunately failed. Brancil was smart, he rammed them using his horns which were now dripping in blood. He stabbed the seven gremlins, two at a time. Now, all of his necklaces had blood on them. Their bodies dropped to the ground as he walked off happily. He found a lot of gems and made 100,431 necklaces. He showed them all to his friends. All of his friends were extremely jealous. Brancil was proud of himself.

Anika Briede (10)
Hart Memorial Primary School, Portadown

The Football Game Of A Lifetime

There is a creature called Billy from Mars. He plays for Handover. Every half-time, he gets subbed on but he plays against Portadown. In the cup final, he gets subbed on for the second half. It was two-one for Portadown. Handover gets a good volley to the top bin and two-two. Portadown is on the attack but Handover stops it. At the 80th minute, Portadown is on the attack again. Billy saves it. Portadown is first for the penalties but it's not in because of Billy. Handover scores. It's one-one. Portadown scores it and wins.

Lukas Kaskonas (10)
Hart Memorial Primary School, Portadown

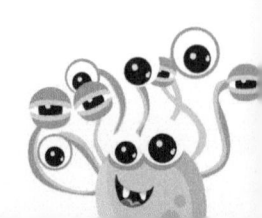

Untitled

One day, a creature from Planet Sharnia decided to explore space so he went to Earth. When he arrived, he landed on a hay bale. Suddenly, he heard footsteps coming so he shape-shifted into a blade of grass. Soon, the thing that aliens call hoo-mins, then walked away. He then decided to prank the hoo-mins so he went to light a field on fire and somehow didn't get caught. Then he took it to a more dangerous situation. So he robbed the bank. He got caught by the police and got arrested. A week later, he disappeared. Or did he?

Taylon Carvalho (10)
Hart Memorial Primary School, Portadown

The Boy Who Went Missing

There was a boy called Michell. He was happy to meet you. Michell was living the life of good parents and a good budget. He could get what he needed, so one day Michell was playing with his toys, and he opened his closet, and he was shocked. He couldn't believe it. A portal was in his closet! Suddenly, a hand stuck out and grabbed his foot tightly, but it let go. Michell breathed in relief. *Boom.* The Boogie Man was there! It put Michell on its shoulder and threw him in the portal, never to be seen again.

Cole Mcandless (10)
Hart Memorial Primary School, Portadown

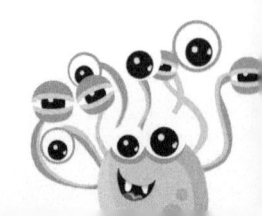

The Malfunction

There once was a planet called Zoink, and a creature called Bonk. One day, Bonk decided to go on a UFO. She flew to Mercury, but a malfunction happened! She was heading the wrong way, she crashed on Earth. She ended up in Portadown! She landed at Hart Memorial. Everyone rushed outside taking photos and videos of Bonk. But one girl called Ella stopped them all! She ran home with Bonk and she tried to help her make a UFO and all the work paid off. Bonk safely flew back to Planet Zoink to see her family. Or did she...?

Emily Magee (9)
Hart Memorial Primary School, Portadown

Pierre The Hero!

Pierre got up in the morning and put the kettle on to make some coffee, but when he opened the fridge, he realised there was no milk left. So off to the shop he went!

As he stood in the queue, he saw two sneaky monsters trying to steal from the store. Just when they thought they had gotten away with it, Pierre managed to trip them up and return the items to their rightful place.

Most people believed monsters were bad, but not Pierre. He was a hero! He was the most clever monster that anyone had heard of.

Ellie-Mae (9)
Hart Memorial Primary School, Portadown

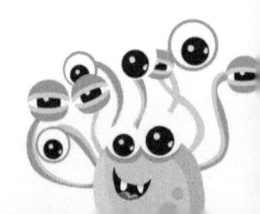

Viggo The Dragon

Viggo was a protective dragon who loved his eggs. But he was a three-headed ice and fire dragon. He flew over the village looking for food. He found some goats grazing. The fearless knight came to Viggo and cut his ice head off. Then, Viggo ran with the goat still in his mouth. Sven, the fearless knight, followed Viggo to his home in the mountains. Sven, the fearless knight, stole the dragon's ice egg (which was the most powerful dragon). He took the dragon and told it what to do and it never saw Viggo again.

Owen Gardiner (9)
Hart Memorial Primary School, Portadown

Max's Revenge

Long ago, there was a dragon called Max. He was a good dragon. He liked fish and meat. He was twenty-one. His girlfriend was called Nelly and her scales were white. They went to the park and found a lonely duck. They loved the duck. It was called Uno. They went to the jungle. They got attacked by a bear. "Oh no!" said Max, as Uno got taken by the bear. Max started to cry as they looked in the jungle. They got taken by the bear. They found Uno. As the bear looked away, they escaped. Happily ever after.

Mia-Louise Craven (9)
Hart Memorial Primary School, Portadown

Untitled

Jiggles is a monster who plays football and he plays keeper. When someone shoots, they don't score because he's big and fat. He will save penalties and free kicks because he blocks the net. Jiggles often gets Man of the Match.

He was going against his enemy, Wiggles, and they were fighting in the match and each got a yellow card. The match was equal and the score was three-all.

When it got to the end they were fighting again, then Jiggles helped Wiggles up at the end and they became friends.

Jayden Watson (9)
Hart Memorial Primary School, Portadown

Jaws Goes Crazy

In the beginning, Jaws was a nice, helpful and playful monster. This was until he developed a fear of loud noises. Every time he heard a loud noise, he'd have an urge to stop it in a nasty way. One day, he crept into school to play games with the children. When he heard children screaming, it made him so angry. He thought the only way to deal with it was to kill them. He ran over to the first victim and tried to eat them. The child slipped away and ran screaming. A helicopter police SWAT team came down.

Jaxon Armstrong (10)
Hart Memorial Primary School, Portadown

The Mission

Me and Victor went on a mission into space. It was going amazingly. We went past the moon and saw the Earth, but then a person attacked us. Victor was really angry, so I had to calm him down. The stranger was trying to get inside the spaceship. I was furious, so Victor jumped out of the spaceship and ripped his hair off. It was a wig! That part was hilarious, but then he got into the spaceship and crashed it. So we took him to the police station and we haven't seen or heard from him since the mission.

Sophie Goncalves (10)
Hart Memorial Primary School, Portadown

The Worst Trip Ever

Once upon a time, a boy named James went on a trip with his parents to go camping. It was in a forest, in the middle of nowhere. They were halfway through the journey in the car but James started to feel a bit sick so his dad stopped the car and parked in the middle of nowhere. James randomly started to vomit and started to feel dizzy until he passed out.

When he woke up, he was in a cave. It was really dark. James started to panic. But he heard a sound until he saw a big *monster*...

Joao Molinet (10)
Hart Memorial Primary School, Portadown

The Crazy Tail

A man was camping when he heard a rattle in the bush. He went to check but nothing was there. So he went back to the fire, but the fire wasn't there. Suddenly, a tail whacked him into a tree. He passed out. When he woke up, he was in a house. A two-tailed cat was standing there. He ran because the door was open. He looked back whilst running and the thing said, "I'll see you soon, David." He was shocked. How did it know his name? But he didn't care, he just needed to run.

Nadia Harhari (9)
Hart Memorial Primary School, Portadown

The Galaxy War

Me and my friend were at the park when suddenly a black hole appeared. We fell in and appeared in Helldoom and became monsters. We were forced to fight for five days. The Devil told us our names. My name was Malatude and his was Unknown. He brainwashed us and gave us powers. We were now enemies and we fought until we died.

We woke up from our sleepover, but a monster took us and it was all the same as the dream that I had and I hated it so much. I never want that to happen ever again.

Lukas Baranovskis (9)
Hart Memorial Primary School, Portadown

The Scare

Breaking news came on the TV while I was watching CITV. An evil elf called Elvin had escaped and was on the run. I got a shock when I opened my bedroom door and saw him under my bed! He said Santa was bad and he was going to kidnap all the children. I told Mummy what he said. Mummy dialled 999 and the police and Mummy explained that he was an evil elf and to always remember that Santa is good. Guess what? On Christmas morning, Santa left me an extra present for facing the evil elf, Elvin.

Sally Steinberg (10)
Hart Memorial Primary School, Portadown

The Disaster Of New York City

Gremlinasaurus was abruptly awoken from his one-thousand-year sleep. He opened his eighteen eyes and clenched his claws.

As he made his way out of his cave, the sight before him was total chaos. People were running and screaming. Bombs were dropping. Gremlinasaurus had no time for this chit-chat. He smashed the helicopters to the ground. He breathed his fiery breath all over the city. Suddenly, there was silence and Gremlinasaurus ruled again! Then he went back to sleep.

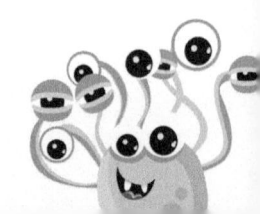

Bobby Woods (10)
Hart Memorial Primary School, Portadown

Rocks On The Tennis Court

Bongo is 20 years old, he likes to play with his best friend, Fred. They both like going on different adventures.

One day, Bongo and Fred were playing crazy tennis again when Big Boy Saga threw a rock onto the tennis court, but Fred didn't fall for it. Big Boy Saga tried again but his plan backfired. He sadly ran away. Fred and Bongo were happy that Big Boy Saga had gone and that he was angry. Bongo and Fred kept playing and had lots of fun. They lived happily ever after.

Ella McCann (10)
Hart Memorial Primary School, Portadown

The Dangerous Alien

The Night Alien went on a journey to Craigavon with his silent pistol. He went into people's houses and went to the bedrooms of the good kids first. He used the silent pistol to shoot the good kids and then dragged the kids to his secret 'dead bodies room'. He put them in there and went back to the bad kids' rooms. He woke them up and forced them to do the same as him. They could not tell anyone or they would be shot with the silent pistol.

Kajus Penkauskas (10)
Hart Memorial Primary School, Portadown

The Unexpected Attack

JimmyJo was having a normal day. He was just walking down the street when he spotted Inky the bully. His plan was to run past him. So JimmyJo started running for his life, but then his shoulder hit Inky. JimmyJo was super scared. Inky put up his fists and punched JimmyJo in the face.
Lazy Larry saw Inky, so he ran away. Then JimmyJo pulled out his banana gun and shot Inky in the head and went home.

Cristovao Azinhais (10)
Hart Memorial Primary School, Portadown

The Great Escape

Once they threw me into the cells of Area 51, I immediately started looking around and I found a screwdriver.
Then, I screwed open the vent in my cell. Next, I started crawling around the vents. After a while, I found the exit.
It was time to use my powers of invisibility to sneak out. After walking miles across the desert, I found the ocean. It was now time to find my family.

Tyler Maguire (9)
Hart Memorial Primary School, Portadown

Goopaw Turns Evil

Goopaw travelled to Planet Earth to get people who dropped litter. He moved super fast and caught people there and then. Once they were captured, he took them to Mars.

When he got to Mars, he let the human he had get absorbed into the goo. He turned into a monster and put Goopaw into the machine. Goopaw turned evil and he went crazy! He tried to destroy Earth.

Danny Crawford (9)
Hart Memorial Primary School, Portadown

Stella And Mrs Summer

Hello, my name is Stella. I live in Bagend. It is a lovely place. I go to Honey Ship School. My favourite teacher is Mrs Summer. I have an electric leg.

One day, I was walking to school. Mrs Summer was trying to teach her class. My electric leg started to zap Mrs Summer. Random things appeared and they fell in and no one ever saw them again.

Macey Oliver (9)
Hart Memorial Primary School, Portadown

What Happened To Dessie?

Once upon a time, there was a girl named Dessie. She was playing at the park with her friends when there was a *boom! Clash! Screech!* Dessie went over to see what was the matter when suddenly, an alien jumped out at her!
All of a sudden, there was a flash of light! Dessie had now turned into a cupcake ghost and had superpowers.

Lucy Roycroft (10)
Hart Memorial Primary School, Portadown

Inky's Revenge

One time, Inky upgraded to fight JimmyJo. It was really hard to find him because he was half the size of Inky. Then JimmyJo jumped on him. Inky became a monster. He was trying to eat JimmyJo. As he was running, he tried to step on him, but he couldn't. Finally, he kicked him and barreled through him. That was karma.

Wojciech Jarosz (9)
Hart Memorial Primary School, Portadown

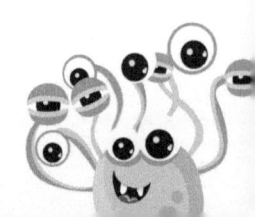

Bob Vs Billy

One day, Bob was rolling after the kids to eat them. He flew after them, but then Billy ate the kids. So Bob bodyslammed Billy and Billy bodyslammed him back and then bit one of his wings off. Don't worry, it will grow back. Then Bob bodyslammed him again and bit Billy's head off.

Caleb Dawson (10)
Hart Memorial Primary School, Portadown

The Tasty Laur Of Jatkala

The local people of Jatkala set off on their mission with one goal: To capture the Laur. The Laur was the most delicious snake for their soup. However, with one bite it could control their mind and kill the whole town. When they started, there was a screech, followed by screams...

Jensen Orr (9)
Hart Memorial Primary School, Portadown

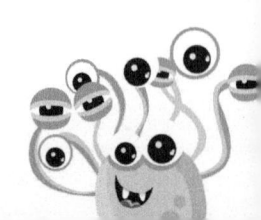

Sprockollie's New Home

After breakfast, John finally persuaded Ginny outside to their beach. They saw an oddly shaped ship on the shore. Out hopped an unusual creature. It had three tongues, fangs and sharp claws. Luckily, his English was fantastic.
"Hi. I'm Sprockollie from outer space. I no longer have a home. Can you help me, please?" John and Ginny were nervous, but they knew the right thing to do was help. They searched high and low. They finally found a beautiful cave with a sea view. Sprockollie was thankful.
John and Ginny heard their mum. "Dinner!" After saying bye, they went home.

George Alperwick (9)
Lakefield CofE Primary School, Gloucester

The Christmas Disaster

Once, Salt and Pepper fell in love. But Vinegarpus stole Salt!

Vinegarpus said, "Salt, listen carefully. You and me will steal Christmas tonight."

But little did Vinegarpus know that Pepper knew about the plan.

So at midnight, Salt and Pepper woke up and made a fire. When Vinegarpus was stealing Christmas, Salt and Pepper pushed Vinegarpus into the fire!

Finally, Christmas was saved.

Then Salt and Pepper went to sleep. They woke up on Christmas Day to heaps of presents.

Later on that day, they had hot cocoa and went ice skating and lived happily ever after.

Lula-Rose Lusty (10)
Lakefield CofE Primary School, Gloucester

The Invisaclops Clash

One day, a didlofier was in a shape-shifting class learning how to shape-shift, but he was bored because he already knew how to shape-shift! Suddenly, an invisaclops smashed the building down. Everybody freaked out apart from Hector. He wasn't scared because he had been in this situation before.

He couldn't handle all of the screaming, so he used his shape-shifting skills and shape-shifted into a little pebble so he could sneak through people's legs. Then, he shape-shifted back into himself and started to fight the invisaclops.

Time passed, and he won the fight.

Sonny Reid (9)
Lakefield CofE Primary School, Gloucester

Blue's Adventure

One day, Blue went on a stroll in the Dark Lake Woods where he lived and a gang of monsters grabbed him and took him to a cave that had chains and bars.

Later that day, a girl called Susie went on a walk by herself and found Blue. "Who are you?" asked Susie.

"I'm Blue, but I work by myself," grunted Blue.

"Okay, bye then," said Susie suspiciously.

"Wait, help!" said Blue.

So they worked together to get him out. He thought the monster's colours were purple, green and yellow so off they went, found them and confronted them.

Connie Fouracres (9)
Lakefield CofE Primary School, Gloucester

Peggy's Mission

Peggy, the one-eyed creature, was talking to her friends at school about humans. She'd read about them in a storybook. Her friend said, "What is a human?"

"They're weird, two-eyed creatures with two legs, no horns and loads of teeth," said Peggy.

At break time, the friends launched over the Jellyfish fence and Peggy jumped into her rocket and blew off into space. The rocket landed on Earth in a zoo. Peggy met a panda and immediately loved it. Thinking it was a human, Peggy placed it in the rocket. The zookeeper jumped in too. Off they blew, home together.

Alice Currie (9)
Lakefield CofE Primary School, Gloucester

The Invasion

Dippy and her friends had a disco with no penguins! When listening to 'Macarena', everyone was loving it, but disaster struck. 106 penguins showed up out of nowhere! Dippy was mad. She scared every penguin except one! That one penguin and Dippy had a massive argument. Then they played 'Gangsta's Paradise'. The noise was so loud; the disco ball broke and fell on the penguin's foot, and the penguin screamed and ran away to safety. Dippy and her friends had a celebration for Dippy, and they danced all night. Everyone enjoyed the rest of the party until the early morning.

Ava Jackson (9)
Lakefield CofE Primary School, Gloucester

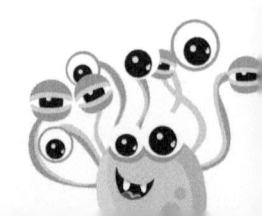

Bonster The Monster

Once, there was a monster called Bonster. She was a gentle but giant monster. She spent every Christmas in the sky, waiting for Santa to arrive. So when Santa came around, Bonster would become invisible and wait for Santa to come at 12 o'clock on the dot. Finally, it was 3am. Bonster looked left. Bonster looked right. Nothing. When she was about to give up, a flash of lights came behind her. She turned around and called, "Santa, look behind. Look behind Santa." Santa suddenly looked behind and chuckled. Suddenly, Bonster woke up. "It was all a dream!" shouted Bonster.

Winnie Price (9)
Lakefield CofE Primary School, Gloucester

Blobbie To The Rescue

Blobbie is an alien from Gzoo but not many people like him because of the slime he leaves.

One day, Blobbie goes for a walk to go to the shops, where he meets Spikey who tells him to go away because of his slime. Suddenly, Spikey drops his keys down a drain. As Blobbie leaves, Spikey shouts for help. Even though Spikey was mean to Blobbie, Blobbie still helps and oozes through the drain and returns Spikey's keys and Spikey says, "Thank you Blobbie."

Blobbie says, "You're welcome."

From that moment on, Blobbie and Spikey become best friends forever.

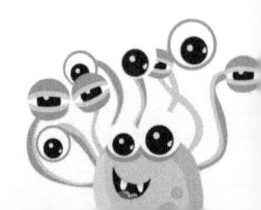

George Price (9)
Lakefield CofE Primary School, Gloucester

The Fairoak Fear

Chloe strolled through Fairoak Forest. Suddenly, a giant, yellow monster with pink spots, antennae like a Chinese dragon and wings of a hawk, swooped down from the darkness of the treetops. Chloe was petrified, but the creature grinned like a Cheshire cat and bowed down, beckoning Chloe to climb onto its back. They took to the skies. Chloe didn't know where they were going but felt safe with the Fairoak Fear. As they descended, Chloe saw flashes of colour. Billions of rainbow Fairoaks played in the meadows below. Chloe loved them so much she happily decided to stay there forever.

Erin O'Gorman-Jevons (9)
Lakefield CofE Primary School, Gloucester

Zlato And Pato

Once upon a time, there were two boys called Zlato and Pato. When Zlato and Pato were walking down the street, a car was in the middle of falling on top of Pato.
Pato said, "Zlato, help!"
Immediately, Zlato sprung into action and said, "I'm coming," and teleported under the car. He used his super strength to pull the car off of Pato, and he did it with everyone watching, jaw-dropped.
Pato said, "Should we go out for some lunch because you saved me?"
The neighbours came out and said, "I know you're the new hero."

William Cabb (9)
Lakefield CofE Primary School, Gloucester

Jasmine And The Dark Angels

The bell went as Jasmine sneaked out of the school building. She darted into the dark forest. "Ouch!" she yelled. *Bang!* She was lying in a bundle in the grass. "Where am I?" She ran to the edge of the woods. "The school's on fire! I'm in the future! I must go back and fight!" She leaped through the gap in the timeline. Suddenly, she saw the Dark Angels. "So they are the ones behind this!" They began to battle - hands clawed each other. This lasted for one whole day but in the end, the Dark Angels were defeated.

Ruby Turner (9)
Lakefield CofE Primary School, Gloucester

The Monster In Sophie's Room

"Sophie!" Mum called to her. "It's time for bed!" Her mum kissed her goodnight then went downstairs. She relaxed her eyes and nearly set off to sleep when she heard a... *clink! Clink! Clink!* sound. Just then, in her sight, was a big, fluffy, blue monster! She tried to scream but she was too nervous. She had to get the monster out of her bedroom before morning. She forced him to leave instantly but he wouldn't so she had to just push him out. Finally, Sophie fell asleep. So, was that all real or was it just another silly dream...?

Clementine Shayle (9)
Lakefield CofE Primary School, Gloucester

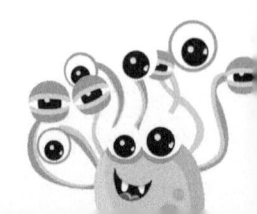

Jeff The Lost Alien

Jeff the Alien was walking in the woods trying to find his way home. He stumbled over and fell down a hole. In the hole was a shadow flickering around. Then, suddenly, there were noises. Out of nowhere was Mr Mole!
Jeff asked, "How can I find my home?"
"There is no way home."
But Jeff noticed a portal behind Mr Mole.
Jeff distracted Mr Mole by saying, "Oh, Mr Mole, look at that yummy worm."
As Mr Mole looked up, Jeff darted to the portal and jumped... landing with a soft bump. He was home and smiled in relief.

Daniel Widgery (9)
Lakefield CofE Primary School, Gloucester

New Shoes For Freddy

Freddy the Fish needed new shoes. The problem was he was a fish with five legs. Buying shoes was hard. The shop wouldn't sell him five shoes, so he always had to buy three pairs and not wear one. Freddy went to the shop. The lady measured his feet, size 53 and a half. She went to see what she had.
"Bad news," she said, "all that we have left in your size are ballet shoes, wellingtons and flip-flops." Freddy was upset but had no choice. He left the shop and wobbled down the road feeling a bit silly.

Esme Peacey (10)
Lakefield CofE Primary School, Gloucester

Too Big For The Bucket

An ordinary family went to the pier with crab lines in anticipation of catching a huge haul of crabs. Before they knew it, one was on the line, they reeled it in. "That's quite small, do we put it in the bucket or do we put it back into the sea?" They decided to put it in the bucket. Suddenly, they heard vibrating coming from the bucket and realised the crab was growing before their eyes. The crab was humongous. They tipped the bucket over into the sea. When it sank down, it started to shrink to its original size.

Poppy Ramsdale (9)
Lakefield CofE Primary School, Gloucester

Scientist Monster

There was a scientist who made a potion. The scientist was adding ingredients to the already blue potion. When he was adding a drop of toxic waste, his belly made the pot wobble and the potion spilt out all over him. The scientist fell straight into a coma where he stayed for a fortnight before turning into a *crazy* creature!
In the blink of an eye, the monster was alive. His name was Cruel Scientist. The monster went on the hunt for food. When he took a bite from a scientist, he turned into a crazy creature.

Harry Knight (9)
Lakefield CofE Primary School, Gloucester

The Monsters Under Your Bed

The monsters who lay under your bed, in your closet, and in your head, the ones who screech out late, to the monsters who give you headaches. Even to the ones that make your brain hallucinate. They all wait until you're asleep to go and haunt your house and dreams. So, we all wonder, what are the beasts' past? Are they refugees from a mysterious land from afar? Why do they stay? Do they have an evil leader to obey? Did they run from a tragic disaster? Or do they do it for fun? They shall remain unknown forever on.

Ben Oliveri (10)
Lakefield CofE Primary School, Gloucester

The Space Creature

There was once a creature called Bob who lived in space. He was planning to go down to Earth and see how it was. He hopped in his spaceship and zoomed down to Planet Earth.
When Bob got there, he was very confused because he had no clue what humans were.
He met a girl called Molly. She started to tell him about humans. She said that humans could be nice and some could be bad.
Molly and Bob became the very best of friends. They started to do everything with each other, and they all lived happily ever after.

Olivia Burrus (9)
Lakefield CofE Primary School, Gloucester

Alien World Vs Real World

Nobbly Nick from the Alien World found a clock. It looked strange so he opened it and he teleported into the real world. It was super strange. They had hot dogs and pretzels. He saw real humans. He didn't fit in at all. He tried and tried and tried. Then he made five friends. But they were animals! Then, all of a sudden, he found he had super speed and was running around everywhere. It was crazy. Next he had sticky feet. He was going up walls and everything. He loved it. His new powers found him loads of friends!

Niamh Rodway (9)
Lakefield CofE Primary School, Gloucester

Quid Quad

He was upset. He was different. He was called Rofus. He was a Ponapede and he was left out and lonely.

There was a competition but there was also a problem. They were one short for the Quid Quad team and Rofus volunteered to play...

The rules of the game were to score as many headers as possible. They found out he was a natural as he had three heads, meaning that he could score three times at once.

Rofus won it for the team! He was a hero and was accepted for who he was, and finally belonged forever!

Chloe Price (10)
Lakefield CofE Primary School, Gloucester

The Eye Octopus

In the valley of Domd, Tom was at the beach with his nineteen sisters and parents. Tom was very excited because he had heard a legend about the Eye Octopus! So he did what any normal person would do and he stole his mum's money. He used it to buy an air tank to go far and deep so he started to swim and swim and swim. Now he was 20,642 kilometres away from shore. He started to go down and down and down. He saw a weird figure in the distance and... he was eaten by the Eye Octopus.

Zac George (10)
Lakefield CofE Primary School, Gloucester

Toothless Gets Home Happy

Toothless was flying through space at the speed of light. Suddenly, an asteroid hit the spaceship. It started to malfunction. He had no choice but to crash-land. He landed in a field on an unknown planet.

There was a sound behind him. He turned around and saw a young boy.

"Do you need help?" said the boy.

"Yes," replied Toothless. They spent all night fixing the spaceship until it finally started again.

"Thank you! I can finally go home," said Toothless.

"Will I see you again?" said the boy.

"Of course," said Toothless. Toothless flew back into space.

Winnie Glossop (8)
New Horizons Primary School, Portsmouth

Snowey's Backstory

One wonderful Friday, Princess Snowey and Princess Siren were playing mermaid tag (before they were enemies). They were having lots of fun. Snowey asked, "Are we going to be friends forever?"
"Yes," replied Siren.
Later that day, Snowey and Siren both found out they both had a crush on Prince Handsome, the most powerful merman on the ocean floor and whoever married him would become the most powerful mermaid on the ocean floor. Snowey loved Prince Handsome for his kindness while Siren loved him for his power. Prince Handsome decided to marry Snowey and that is how they became enemies.

Dara Sonubi (9)
New Horizons Primary School, Portsmouth

Rosie's New Friend

One boring Saturday, Rosie was thinking of something to do. She had an idea. She wandered into the woods. As she was passing by, there was a sudden sound of rustling in the bushes. Rosie was startled. "Who's there?" she stuttered. She looked closer. A furry and pink creature shot out of the bush like fireworks. Rosie got frightened. "What and who are you?" she asked.

There was a long silence. You could hear a pin drop. The creature spoke. "Sorry for scaring you. I'm Chloe. I'm from Wonderwood."

After their conversation, they became very good friends.

EwaogoOluwa Adefioye (9)
New Horizons Primary School, Portsmouth

A Friend In The End

Eric is my monster, my bestie, and my neighbour. Pheobe owns a monster too. Normally, both of them hate and despise each other.

Today was different. I took Eric to Pheobe's house even though he begged me to stay home. I put Eric down and Jake chased him into the garden. When they couldn't hear, Pheobe said she had put cameras everywhere.

When Jake had caught up with Eric, he started bawling.

"Please, stop it! Please can we be friends?" he sobbed.

Eric pondered for a minute. "Sure," he replied.

Eric ran to me. "Megan, I've got a new friend.

Megan Browning (10)
New Horizons Primary School, Portsmouth

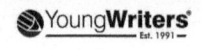

Oddball

India wasn't excited. She just moved from the Indian Ocean to the Pacific Ocean. She was worried, very worried that she would be the odd one out. "Hello?" India asked politely. She didn't notice all the identical monsters giggling at her. "Haha, you're weird-looking. You can't be here!" Winnie laughed.
"Well, I can! Just because you look 'perfect' doesn't mean we aren't all perfect the way we are!" India yelled gracefully.
All the monsters shouted, "Yeah!" They all changed to their real looks.

Maddie-May Nash (9)
New Horizons Primary School, Portsmouth

Sapphire Moon

Once upon a time, there was a monster. Her name was Sapphire Venus Moon. She lived on Venus but was born on the moon. She could turn into a person. Everybody thought that she was different. She had one friend who lived on Mars so they never got to see each other.

One day, Sapphire went to visit Jesse. Suddenly, Sapphire bumped into the Princess of Mars. "Why are you here?" shouted Savana. Savana walked away and so did Sapphire. Jesse loved Sapphire so Jesse told Sapphire that he loved her. Suddenly, Savana came and told Sapphire to go home.

Phoebe Neary (9)
New Horizons Primary School, Portsmouth

Peter Goes On Holiday

Peter was nine and from the USA. He was going on holiday to the UK to visit London. His enemy, Red-Eye, was trying to stop Peter from going on holiday, as it would mean he wouldn't have anyone. Red-Eye often stopped people from doing fun things!

Hooray! The day came for Peter to pack his bags, but Red-Eye kept unpacking Peter's bag and hiding his clothes. Peter noticed what Red-Eye was doing. Red-Eye repacked Peter's bag. Unknowingly, Peter put Red-Eye into his bag and got on the plane. They both really enjoyed themselves.

Harrison Winmill (8)
New Horizons Primary School, Portsmouth

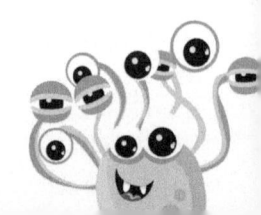

Stephanie's Story

Once there was a creature named Stephanie. Stephanie was indestructible so she was able to live on Venus (the hottest planet in the solar system). Stephanie wasn't the only one that lived on Venus. Loads of other creatures lived there too. A year later, she found out that she was going to have to move to Earth in a month and her enemy Jake was going too! When she arrived on Earth and was settled in, she got into a school. She got her uniform ready. The next Monday, she arrived at school. Sadly, she got bullied. DO NOT BULLY!

Lucy Holden (9)
New Horizons Primary School, Portsmouth

The Monster Who Got Bullied

In the morning, Eye-Bat the monster, was at break time at school. He saw his enemy coming up to him. He was terrified. His enemy said, "I'm going to beat you up after school." When he came in for a maths lesson, he was nervous to tell his teacher about it. After school, there he was, the enemy. He tried punching Eye-Bat but Eye-Bat used his skills so he could see where he was going to punch him. Then he ran away to his majestic house. His mum saw it all and Eye-Bat isn't allowed to use his skills outside.

Tomasz Wygowski (9)
New Horizons Primary School, Portsmouth

A New Friend For Megan

Once upon a time, there was a little girl called Megan. One day, she was feeling brave and decided to take a walk in the deep, dark forest and got chased by the undead. She ran for ages but when they all got tired, Megan sat wheezily by a tree and the undead went back underground, except for one. And Megan walked over and gave it some food and turned out to be friendly so they played together whilst the hours raced by until Megan decided to go home but Deevil didn't wanna leave her. So Megan took her home.

Anya Mitchell (9)
New Horizons Primary School, Portsmouth

The Hatching Of Actrozilla

Once in a lifetime, an unknown species landed on Planet Earth due to a collision from a different planet. According to scientists, the creature was making ear-piercing screeches. The peculiar species vanished and left a trace of a strange type of glue in a matter of seconds. A mysterious beam came out of the sky and hit Actrozilla and became bigger and bigger until it became huge and destroyed many cities. The government had enough so they got all of the military equipment to end this once and for all!

Patrik Dascalescu (9)
New Horizons Primary School, Portsmouth

The Last Thing Alive?

Brown Bunny emerged. It was silent. "Where's my brother? Where is everyone?" The last thing Brown Bunny could remember was the earth shaking. Then darkness. Brown Bunny felt completely alone, but he wasn't. Googol wasn't like anything he'd seen before. He had eight eyes and eight legs. He looked scary. Brown Bunny was afraid. From behind Googol stepped his brother, Black Bunny. "Where did you come from?" asked Brown Bunny. "Can you help us find our sister, White Bunny?" they pleaded.
Googol paused. "I can save everybody." Together, they set off to save the world. One bunny at a time...

James Hemmings (9)
Springwell Park Community Primary School, Bootle

Shadow Fang: The Friendly Football Star

Shadow Fang has one eye and is known as a talented football player. Despite his intimidating appearance, he's actually really friendly and has tonnes of friends. He loves hanging out with his monster buddies, both on and off the football field. Shadow Fang has infectious energy and is a member of the Monster High Community. Whether he's scoring goals or cheering on his teammates, Shadow Fang always brings excitement to Monster High School. He has horns on top of his head. Everyone loves them and his football skills, goals and kindness. He hasn't any differences towards other people that aren't popular.

Erika Domnitanu (9)
Springwell Park Community Primary School, Bootle

The Alien Battle!

Once upon a time, Eagcorn was relaxing in his spotty hammock. Then Professor John Bob ambushed him. Then Eagcorn said, "You!"
And Professor John Bob replied, "You think you can send me to Mars?"
And Eagcorn said back, "Maybe?" Then he went into action! Then Professor John Bob did too! So then they fought each other until they were both so tired and aching. So they said, "What is the point in being enemies? We should just be happy and be friends!"
So they became friends and also they forgot that they had to clean up the mess they made.

Ella Rowley (9)
Springwell Park Community Primary School, Bootle

Tom Goes To The Park

Tom wants to go to the park. "Mummy, can we go to the park please?" asks Tom.
"Yes, let's go to the park. Come on," replies Mum. Tom and his mum are going to the park. When they arrive at the park, Tom meets his friend Sarah. "Hi, Sarah!" shouts Tom.
"Hi, Tom!" replies Sarah.
"Let's go and play together," says Sarah. So they go to go and play together on the monkey bars. A few minutes later, they go back home.

Vanessa Wezyk (9)
Springwell Park Community Primary School, Bootle

The Lost Alien

Once upon a time, there was an alien called Mobo. He was kicked from his home planet and sent to Earth. His ship was fine but he felt dizzy. He saw a TV, it said that his planet was going to be destroyed. He was going back to his planet to tell everyone what was going on but when he got there, the guards wouldn't let him in. They wouldn't listen to him! Will he save the planet and everyone on it?

Charlie Jones (10)
Springwell Park Community Primary School, Bootle

The Giant Fart Doodle

The Giant Fart Doodle is too windy, plus he's in King's Nooze. That's miles away. You'll have to go on an aeroplane if you want to defeat the Giant Fart Doodle, but apart from that, how will you defeat the Giant Fart Doodle?
"A sword on an aeroplane?"
"My hands?"
"So you are going to take your hands off?"
"No, I mean like hit him, punch him, kick him."
"An animal."
"Wait, it's an animal you say."
"Yes, what of course he is."
"It's a monster flamingo. You do know that a flamingo is an animal right?"
"Yes, of course."

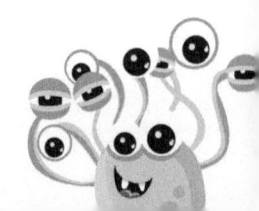

William Madl (8)
St Agnes' Catholic Primary School, Crawcrook

Untitled

Jeff lives on Planet Zong Cong. He has to go to battle with his enemy, Captain Hairly. He is so mad at his boss, but he goes to Earth to battle, gets his guns, and goes. Captain Hairly is already there and starts to shoot, but Jeff fights back. He shakes a truth pill, and Captain Hairly says, "I'm your mother."
Shocked, he says, "Are you really?"
She says, "Yes."
They both say, "Sorry."
She says, "I've missed you so much, and sorry I tried to shoot you. Let's go home together and be friends forever."
They live together.

Neve Ball (8)
St Agnes' Catholic Primary School, Crawcrook

The Lonely Monster

Outside, in the dark, gloomy forest was a lonely monster. In shock, he saw smoke like people were camping! Monster started teleporting towards the smoke. Suddenly, Monster was there and everyone started to run away. Lonely Monster sadly went to a tree and sat there. Monster was thinking, *why is everyone scared of me?* Monster suddenly saw another monster trying to scare more people. Monster tried to scare people so the Monster would come see him. And he did. So Monster started scaring more people with all of the other monsters. Now, Lonely Monster has friends. He is very happy.

Thomas Rafferty (8)
St Agnes' Catholic Primary School, Crawcrook

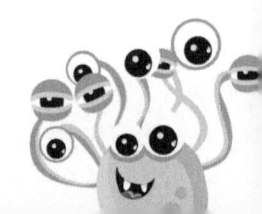

The Fearful Monster

The weird monster with six eyes approached the city with fearful fangs. Everyone was running for their lives knowing that no one was safe.
There was a flash, then a bang. The monster hunters were there, defeating the monster and getting everyone to safety. Still, the monster didn't give up, as he ate one big skyscraper, getting bigger and bigger until the six-eyed monster was huge. All the monster hunters went around the monster three to one. They threw the net over the monster. Everyone was celebrating and clapping. There were huge high-fives.
Job done monster hunters.

Isabelle Batsford (8)
St Agnes' Catholic Primary School, Crawcrook

School Strikes Again

As Stella looked down from Wachway Planet, she saw Salway's School's headmaster giving each student sweets. She could smell trouble so she flew down to Earth. She turned invisible and went to the office. She heard that the headmaster wanted to sweeten up the kids so she could eat them! Stella tried to control her mind but it didn't work! She checked her watch. "No! Mum put mind controlling off so I would do my homework!" She remembered she could hack it. Pull and turn. She mind-controlled the headmaster so she wouldn't eat the kids. Bravo! Bravo! Job done.

Clara Cantrill (9)
St Agnes' Catholic Primary School, Crawcrook

The Two-Headed Sister

One day, in the middle of June, the two-headed sister came out of hiding. She started causing havoc in the town of Calander. Then, the kind-hearted sister appeared and challenged her. They fought and fought before running around the town again and again. The two-headed sister hit but the kind-hearted sister fought with words. The kind-hearted sister said, "We don't have to fight." But the other sister wouldn't listen. So the kind-hearted sister got out her love arrow. She poised herself and shot. The two-headed sister collapsed, defeated. A good job well done!

Phoebe Catterall (9)
St Agnes' Catholic Primary School, Crawcrook

Bangidash

My creature came back from winning a fight again, against Libidy Blob Blob by using lightning bolt arms. But just as he was walking home, his lightning bolt arms fell off and someone was there. *But who was it?* Libody Blob Blob thought. "It couldn't be Libidy Blob Blob," he said to himself. So he asked, "Who are you?" in Hoti language.
He said, "No response." Because he ran away. He used a portal to get to Planet Hot on time to make more research about that guy and make some more shiny, gold, beautiful, lightning bolt-shaped arms.

Ethan Richardson (8)
St Agnes' Catholic Primary School, Crawcrook

The Adventure Begins

One day, Bearipus was having a dream and it felt so real. In the dream, he was on a falling meteor. The meteor fell all the way to Earth. When it got to Earth, Bearipus met a bear called Blue. Blue was, as a matter of fact, blue. Blue had ears just a bit smaller than Bearipus, a large brown nose and a small mouth.
Blue introduced himself by saying, "I'm Blue, the blue polar bear."
He looked as if he had an old, raggedy necktie.
Blue asked, "Who are you?"
Bearipus replied, "I'm Bearipus from the Meteor Planet."

Imogen Rodgers (8)
St Agnes' Catholic Primary School, Crawcrook

822-Experiment

In Crankroot, there was a flash and a monster appeared. His name was 822-Experiment. He sneezed and bouncy balls shot from his mouth. He could jump as high as a skyscraper. There was another flash. 822-Experiment knew who this was. It was his nemesis, Nightman, who wanted to capture him to use his powers for evil. 822-Experiment ran into the chip shop. Nightman went to every shop but one. He must be in there. He ran into the chip shop, but 822-Experiment used his bouncy balls, making him fall, giving 822-Experiment time to call his friends to beam him home.

Theo Sage (8)
St Agnes' Catholic Primary School, Crawcrook

Peace Once Again

The world was a happy and joyful place until the hunters came. They trooped out and killed twenty-five bunnies, cats, ducks and birds. A buzzer soon went off on Planet Catbunbiuck and Catabun was sent to stop the hunters. Catabun flew down and assembled an army of bunnies, cats, birds and ducks. Then they set a trap where the hunters fell in. Catabun was pleased. Together, the birds destroyed the guns and made the hunters say, "We're very sorry."
Catabun said, "Come back to us, friends."
So the animals rose and they lived.

Jessica Slegg (8)
St Agnes' Catholic Primary School, Crawcrook

Funny Candy To The Rescue

This adventure starts at Hamleys, a well-known toy shop. Funny Candy gets a toy aeroplane and flies it outside, but while it's flying, it grows into a real-sized aeroplane! Funny Candy gets in it and flies over the Tower Of London. She sees Yummy Veg with the Crown Jewels! She swoops the aeroplane to the ground, runs to Yummy Veg, trips him over, grabs the Crown Jewels and gives them to a guard, saying, "Yummy Veg stole these; I'm returning them."
The guard tells the King and Funny Candy gets a lifetime supply of yummy candy.

Annabelle Slegg (8)
St Agnes' Catholic Primary School, Crawcrook

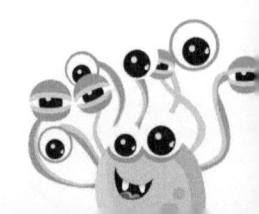

Warden Vs Gummy King

The Warden is a monster king! He has a hole in the middle of his body, horns sticking out of his head, triangular eyes and he's blue. He wants to eat the gummy with his big mouth. He needs to travel to Cloudy Land where Gummy King lives. He gets off on his adventure! He walks along Gummy Road, under candyfloss clouds, swims through Nutella River, climbs Frutella Mountain and runs through Smartie raindrops. Arriving at the throne, starting to fight using sharp claws, he defeats Gummy King, making him into little gummy bears for him to eat. Yummy!

Isaac Beading (8)
St Agnes' Catholic Primary School, Crawcrook

The Acidic Mission

One day, a Mirrorer was on Earth for a mission assigned by the king. Soon, it found its mission: a human was getting dragged by another Mirrorer! Mirrorer One had to do something. It leapt for the possessed Mirrorer, knowing it because the Mirrorer had a purple eye. After the possessed Mirrorer was stunned, he grabbed the human by the hips and flew away. The ghost who was possessing the Mirrorer left the body and said, "You're no use. I've failed him."
The human thanked the hero Mirrorer for saving him and the king cheered.

Isaac Mason Burnett (8)
St Agnes' Catholic Primary School, Crawcrook

Blobby And The Monsters!

Down in the depths of a dark tunnel, in King Snoose town, lived the most scary, stinky, slimy and cleverest monster called Blobby. He wasn't always a good monster as everything he touched was slimy and stinky. One day, Blobby comes out of his tunnel. He never does because he is scared of the other monsters. he hears something coming from space with his super slime senses. There is a meteorite heading to Earth! Blobby uses his body to shield the Earth from the meteorite. He saves the world and now he is the hero of the whole entire Earth.

Mia Blake (8)
St Agnes' Catholic Primary School, Crawcrook

Weirdwalker And The Prime Minister's Pants

Weirdwalker was hiding when a shiny limo sped past. This must be someone important! If he could capture them, the world would know his strength! He couldn't do it with his usual stomping... He slowly transformed his feet, so they were tiny as a ladybird. Now, he could creep up on them without being seen. He shot out a vine at the nearest man - the Prime Minister - who jumped in shock as his pants fell down! Weirdwalker was exhausted and in that moment, a cat leapt in and used its claws to slash through the vines, releasing the prisoners!

Emily Williams (8)
St Agnes' Catholic Primary School, Crawcrook

Long Arms Saves The Day Again

In Scotland, on Haggis Street, Nancy, who was ten, fell asleep in her very comfy bed and amazingly floated off into space to a planet called Amerphia. Luckily for Nancy, the one and only Long Arms caught a glimpse of Nancy bouncing over to the evil Short Arms' planet nearby where Short Arms was ready to take her DNA to make her evil too and take over the world. Just then, Long Arms wrapped his fantastically humongous elastic-type of arms around her and pulled her safely back to Earth's surface where she fell into her comfy bed.

Ed Johnson (8)
St Agnes' Catholic Primary School, Crawcrook

Big Mouth Vs Little Mouth

Down in the royal garden, Big Mouth is talking to the flowers. He hears Sunflower crying and goes to see what is wrong. She can see the future and says, "Evil Little Mouth is on his way to steal the king's plants and jewels." Big Mouth prepares for the attack. Big Mouth asks the plants to call in all the bees. The bees swarm in and huddle up. As Little Mouth reaches the royal garden, Big Mouth shouts, "Attack!" The bees then sensationally form a bee torpedo and chase him away. The garden is at peace once again.

Thea Exley (8)
St Agnes' Catholic Primary School, Crawcrook

Goolu's Secret Chamber

A family, a mum, dad, brother and a little monster called Goolu. They were in bed and heard a loud, strong crash! All of them jumped up and saw the planet Mars had crashed into their island. It was smashed into little pieces. The planet lit up on fire. Their dad said, "Run!" They went through their little house, all the way to the Chamber of Secrets. There, they found a water trident, and all of them held onto it. It spread the water around the island and brought the wonderful little island back together. They lived happily.

Ella Williams (8)
St Agnes' Catholic Primary School, Crawcrook

Planet Bippo Is In Trouble

There was once a planet called Planet Bippo and it was in danger. The planet was in a faraway galaxy surrounded by thousands of other planets. One day, Goo Goo Master decided to attack Planet Bippo because he wanted to be King of the Universe. King Cherry of Planet Bippo wasn't having any of it so he sent his most deadliest monster to stop Goo Goo and his minions. So Slinkfang stopped Goo Goo and his minions pretty much then. Slinkfang did something terrible that he would never do again. He sent Goo Goo and his minions to Earth.

Phoebe Stephenson (9)
St Agnes' Catholic Primary School, Crawcrook

Rico's Win

It's the National Sprint Championships in San Piricio. Rico makes new friends, chatting with the other athletes. The race starts and Rico is in the lead. At the halfway mark, he trips on his long arm and ends up doing a backflip. He wipes out all the other athletes. Rico stands back up and dashes for the finish line. He trips again and does his first-ever front flip over the finish line. He wins the race! He collects his golden trophy and his new friends clap and cheer. He happily lifts the golden trophy up high in the air.

Reuben Roberts (9)
St Agnes' Catholic Primary School, Crawcrook

The Unhappy Monster

The creature watches over the monsters below. He is one of the best guards ever. He is disappointed. He is a monster, not a human. He would do anything to be human. He does not like fighting. If he ever sees a human, he gets upset, even though he will not get cool powers like flying or becoming invisible, he still just wants to be a normal human. So he travels to a mysterious wood in the middle of nowhere where no people go. The creature is never seen again. Everyone searches but never finds him or the mysterious human.

Kristian Hutchinson (8)
St Agnes' Catholic Primary School, Crawcrook

The Legend Of Gostopous

One boy was tucked up in bed but the gostopous took him so in a flash they went to Gozland. When they got there, the boy was still asleep in his blanket so the gostopous waited and waited until it was dawn. But the next day, the boy brought a ball so the gostopous was curious but the boy said, "Do you want to play football?" Then the boy got to his feet and the boy trained Goz. But then it was getting late so Goz ran back to the boy's house. His mum was terrified, so was his dad.

Finlay Curry (8)
St Agnes' Catholic Primary School, Crawcrook

The Monster's Revenge

This monster will bite if interacted with so do not go in its path or else you will get sonic boomed and you are not going to be able to dodge.
Since all his friends died, he wants to get revenge on all humans. So he taught himself to be so strong. He is unbeatable. He has no weaknesses and will not die from age. Even his bat will not die. He is unbeatable as well.
One big secret is that he adores dogs and is very kind to them. Even though he wants one, everyone is around, so mad.

Emile Goss (9)
St Agnes' Catholic Primary School, Crawcrook

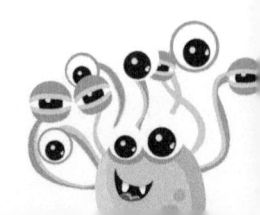

Jaffa's Power!

There once lived a creature that lived in Blobville. He had the power of shape-shifting into anything he wanted, but Jaffa didn't use his power rightly; he used it for bad things!

One day, Jaffa woke up and tried to shape-shift, but he couldn't! Jaffa thought he was doomed but then called his friend, Potator, who also lived in Blobville. Potator didn't help, so he called his friend, Bostoona.

His best friend said to him, "You don't need a power to be Jaffa; the real Jaffa would say the same thing."

Jaffa lived on without powers!

Zainab Qayum (10)
St Mark's CofE Primary School, Stoke-On-Trent

The Bullied Monster

Once a monster named Rose went to school in Monstertopia.

At school, a few monsters bullied and teased her. When Rose got back home, she went to her room and cried. When Rose's mum came into her room, she asked Rose why she was crying. Rose said that the monsters were bullying her. Her mum told Rose to be brave and to tell the monsters to stop bullying her.

At school the next day, the monsters bullied Rose. But Rose told the monsters not to bully her or else she would tell the teacher. Then Rose became the monsters' friend.

Fatimah Zaheer (10)
St Mark's CofE Primary School, Stoke-On-Trent

The Scary Monster With Lots Of Eyes

There was a scary monster who scared every child and the adult people were saying he was really strange, but he didn't care. So he was always smiling at people. Little babies liked playing with him. He seemed really funny to babies, but one thing was that at night he went to people's houses and scared them. When it was night he glowed in the dark. He had lots of eyes, like ten eyes! That was why people got scared of him. He was my favourite character. He was a really scary, crazy creature. He had long teeth.

Ana-Maria Mitran (10)
St Mark's CofE Primary School, Stoke-On-Trent

Crazy Eye Creature

The five-eye creature had an enemy and their home was miserable. Then they had a fight and they were both bleeding badly. The five-eye creature had killed Mikecrasky because it threw Mikecrasky off a high, dangerous, rocky cliff.

Mason Paul Buxton (10)
St Mark's CofE Primary School, Stoke-On-Trent

Bunny Bubble's First Christmas

One icy, cold winter's day, Bunny Bubble was drastically bored, so decided to fly to Earth and cause havoc among humans.

Bunny Bubble was a naughty creature, who stole children's happiness. Whilst taking a stroll along the woods, she bumped into another alien called Christmas Butterfly.

"What are you doing here?" exclaimed Bunny Bubble.

"I'm delivering Christmas presents to all the children. It's Christmas Eve. Do you want to help me?"

Bunny Bubble was shocked and surprised. She believed it was Santa all along. She was amazed and decided to be a better alien this year. More giving and generous.

Jaslena Manka (8)
St Mary's School, Gerrards Cross

Wish Catastrophe

On a sunlit day, Sasha leaned back on her chair as she groaned. Her blue hair tumbled down her shoulder like a waterfall. It was maths and Sasha disliked it. *If only I could wish my way out, although I don't want to break my New Year's Resolution*, she thought.

At break, Sasha, performed 'acceptably' through maths however she ended up hiding in the toilet. "Hey," said a firm voice. "Gimme some of your 'magical' wishes."

Oh no, thought Sasha. It was her sister Lasha, who always yearned for her wishes. Sasha saw Lasha's friends behind her. She couldn't run!

Jahnavi Misra (11)
St Mary's School, Gerrards Cross

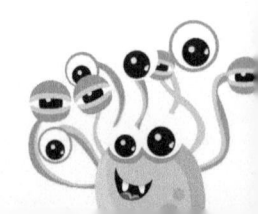

Bump In The Night

Zoo has never seen daylight before because she lives under April's bed. Zoo is a wisdom creature although she has a secret; she is afraid of humans. One night, a peculiar noise came from under April's bed in the dead of night. *Screech. Screech.* April woke up in shock and peered under her bed. All she could see was a black shadowy figure. Suddenly, the creature started to run around frantically. As it was startled it ran into the bookshelf and the books thumped on the wooden floor. Just then, they made eye contact. Surprisingly, like looking into a mirror.

Ishani Dhamecha (10)
St Mary's School, Gerrards Cross

Walking

One calm day, Input was walking through the dark Himalayan mountains. After five long, boring hours, he met Bogal Weard who was his best friend.
"Are you coming to the party at the top of the Himalayan mountain?" asked Bogal Weard.
"Yes, I am," replied Input.
After two hours, Input went to the party at the top of the Himalayan mountains, but before he could reach the top, he saw Mumblybow, his enemy. So he crept behind a boulder and rolled it where he had walked.
After some time, he reached the party. "Whoo!" Input cried.

Jayna Master (8)
St Mary's School, Gerrards Cross

Honey's Honey

Honey was a bee-bear hybrid, and she liked to make honey.
One day, Honey wanted to make some honey. First, she found a tree with a hive. Then she started to climb. Up she went, hanging onto each branch tightly. Finally, she got there. As she clung to the last branch, a small bee stung her! Immediately, the whole swarm started to sting her aggressively, going in deep to create a gorge in her skin. Suddenly, she fell down onto the floor with a *THUMP*. Honey had not succeeded, so she rolled her eyes and humphed a big "Humph..."

Jaya Bass (10)
St Mary's School, Gerrards Cross

The Day At The Park

One day I was at the fun park when I saw a beautiful monster on the slide. She started walking closer, and then she asked if I would be her friend. I said "Yes" and found out her name was Millie.
"I really like your angel wings. They're sparkling like gold."
Then we went on the slide, but unfortunately, Millie got stuck, so I went down the slide and pushed her the rest of the way. We had ice cream to make her feel better.
But then I realised that I had saved the day.

Katie Donaghey (8)
St Mary's School, Gerrards Cross

The Creepy Monster From Neptune

One day there was a little boy who wanted to go to space. He went downstairs and asked his mum, "Can I make a rocket?"
"No, because your dinner is ready."
So he finished his dinner and rushed upstairs. Suddenly, he saw a big, purple creature with ten arms and three eyes!
"Who are you?"
"My name is Ted," said the creature.
"Nice to meet you. Where are you from?"
"I'm from Neptune," replied the creature.
Soon after, Mum came upstairs and said, "Time for bed, darling."
So the creature hid in Jacob's closet and sang a space lullaby.

Freya Hill (11)
St Michael's CE (VC) Junior School, Twerton

Crazy Creatures

One day, there was a girl called Phoebe. She went to her local shop.
When she was walking back home, she saw something weird. So she went up to the creature and then she ran all the way to her house. Then she called her friend and said, "Hide somewhere!" Then Phoebe hung up.
Then the monster was gone, so Phoebe thought it was safe, and it was safe, so everyone went out. Then it was all very safe, and they did not know what had happened to the weird creature that was very scary.

Jessica Rose Hill (10)
St Michael's CE (VC) Junior School, Twerton

Friends In Space

Squelch! A rocket lands on the Cheddar moon. As the door opens an excited girl named Jenny leaps from the rocket and begins to explore the mysterious moon. "Aaahhh!" Jenny screams as she spots Furby, a big scary monster peeking behind a lump of Cheddar, with purple fur, five googly eyes and three twig legs. Jenny is petrified and quickly hides. Furby begins to cry. She is sad that Jenny finds her terrifying. Jenny hears Furby crying and bravely goes to comfort her. They spend all day playing and eating cheese. They become the best of friends.

Autumn Reardon (7)
St Robert Bellarmine Catholic Primary School, Bootle

The Day Izzy Found A Friend

One day, Izzy went to school, and Bell came up to her and was mean. Bell walked away with her friends, laughing so loudly. Izzy was lonely because all the children were scared to play with her because of Bell, and that hurt.
Izzy was in Year 3 like me!
One day later, a new student came in. His name was Jack. Jack liked Izzy because she looked kind, and they became good friends.
Bell wanted to be friends with them. Izzy told Bell, "If you want to be friends with us, stop being mean to the other children."

Emily Powell (7)
St Robert Bellarmine Catholic Primary School, Bootle

The Moon Monster

Zack the monster had three legs and seven eyes and he was so hungry but he was allergic to water. So he only wanted food. He met an eight-year-old. Her name was Lilly and Zack wasn't allergic to anything any more, so he wasn't hungry any more because the little girl, Lilly, had lots of food for him to eat. So Zack had a friend called Lilly. Then he fixed the spaceship and flew back to the moon. Before that he said, "Thank you for helping me," and gave her a big hug.
Lilly said, "Bye."

Scarlett Green (7)
St Robert Bellarmine Catholic Primary School, Bootle

Shadow Vs Light

One day, Shadow was flying up in the sky but then Light appeared! He started shooting Light spares! But Shadow attacked back with Shadow fires. Light was burned super bad but after that, Light went into his final form which gave him four tentacles and a x20 power boost after a long time of getting hurt, Shadow got his final form with 4 Shadow tentacles and a +21 power boost. Shadow got an Uno reverse card. When he got it, Light was about to kill Shadow then he pulled the Uno reverse card and killed Light instead.

Dylan Hurley (8)
St Robert Bellarmine Catholic Primary School, Bootle

An Adventure

Once upon a time, there were two cousins named Bella and Jasmine. One day, they were very bored, so they decided to go to Planet Marshy. They discovered horpups, but there was not just one, there were millions. One was really kind and generous, so it came home with Bella and Jasmine. As they went to sleep, Bella said to Jasmine, "That was an incredible day!"

"I know," said Jasmine to Bella, and they all lived happily ever after.

Jasmine Wilson (8)
St Robert Bellarmine Catholic Primary School, Bootle

Ollie And The Yeti

Once there was a monster called Ollie. He was sunbathing, but then the yeti came along and they had a massive fight. It was amazing. They both got injured, but in the end, Ollie won.
Ollie tried so hard, he got a world record, and the yeti died, so Ollie went to the funeral and said, "I didn't try to kill you."
And Ollie went back to sunbathing.

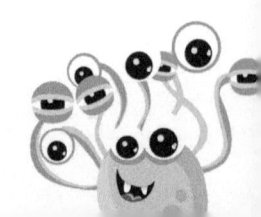

Archie Owens (7)
St Robert Bellarmine Catholic Primary School, Bootle

Speedy Silky Going On A Run

A little monster, Silky, went on a run. Suddenly, an alarm came. There was a little girl sitting on the hills crying from the inside, normal from the outside. Silky asked, "What's the alarm for?"
On, off. The monsters escaped.
"What should we do? She's a dangerous monster! We have to avoid her at all costs!"
It was too late, the monsters came and went to destroy the only house in the woods, Silky's house. The girl and Silky charged up and destroyed the monster. The monster called Belinda died with a punch. The girl joined the battle and won.

Anaya Taher (10)
St Silas CE Primary School, Blackburn

Aliemon And Aliecon

Aliemon, who was sitting on his chair, was eating his delicious ice ball. Suddenly he sensed that his rude stinky brother was coming. Aliecon, his brother came in. His brother threw an ice ball at him. Aliemon dodged it. He used his invisibility power. Aliemon sneaked up behind him, and Aliecon swiftly looked around. He couldn't sense where his sneaky brother was. Aliemon smacked Aliecon's face. He threw several ice balls at him. He threw his brother out of his house with his insane overpowered superstrength. He could live in happiness... for now, he thought.

Daniyal Ahmed (9)
St Silas CE Primary School, Blackburn

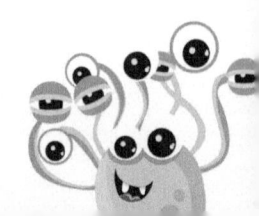

Bubbles Saves The Day!

One day, Spicker the pufferfish came to terrorise the world. Bubbles saw this on the news down at the Great Barrier Reef. She thought of saving all of the citizens, so that's what she did. Swimming up to the Great Barrier Reef and using her power, she was able to stop Spicker from doing his madness. They became friends.
Bubble said to Spicker, "Come over for tea at the Great Barrier Reef."
Spicker said, "Yes, of course."
They played together, started doing everything together, and the people remembered this day ever since.

Fatima Patel (9)
St Silas CE Primary School, Blackburn

Belinda Saves The World

One morning, Belinda decided to have a walk down the street. She took some money to buy a few things. While Belinda was walking, she saw some soil on the ground and ran away. Belinda was scared of soil because it made her dirty.
Belinda went to the shop and didn't see any food.
"I wonder what has happened to all the soil?" said the shop's owner.
"All of the world's soil is mine!" Silky came in and shouted.
Belinda ran towards the box with all the soil.
Belinda then told the people to take soil. She saved the day!

Haadiya Saifullah (9)
St Silas CE Primary School, Blackburn

Mr Smelly Pants

Mr Smelly Pants's skills are shape-shifting and teleportation. He is from South Korea. His enemies are people who hate K-pop, but Mr Smelly Pants loves K-pop so much.

One day, Mr Smelly Pants decides to destroy his enemies' house. He knows where their house is and where the K-pop haters live together. Even the K-pop haters know where his house is, so he shape-shifts into a human and teleports to their house.

As he goes to their house in one click, the house is destroyed. When the K-pop haters enter the house, they are scared when it opens.

Aliya Nisar (10)
St Silas CE Primary School, Blackburn

The Scary Dragon!

The Scary Dragon was destroying the cars and cities to rob the bank. He made a tsunami to stop me, to rob the bank. Then a big creature came called Dino Danny, he was a good character. He came to stop the tsunami and stop the creature named Scary Dragon. Dino Danny used his powers to stop the tsunami but he couldn't because Scary Dragon was much too strong but Dino Danny didn't give up. He had an idea to destroy Scary Dragon. He called his friends for help. His friend came and destroyed the scary dragon once and forever.

Affan Usman (10)
St Silas CE Primary School, Blackburn

Cobre Kai

Dragon Bull Zee fought a farm and destroyed it. He came to help the farm; his name was Speedy, and he helped the farm. His skills were breathing out fire, and he had his sticky pads on. Dragon got angry because he wanted a pen from a school. He broke them because he was desperate for a pen. Finally, he got a pen, then he felt sorry for the teacher. All of the kids stole the pen.
The Dragon said, "Give them back."
But they didn't give them back, then he shouted, and the Dragon felt sorry for the children.

Daniyal Miah (9)
St Silas CE Primary School, Blackburn

Fluffy Monster's Life

Fluffy Monster is from Neptune. His skills are jumping really high. His enemies are sharks and dolphins. His friend is Asp 1932. One day Fluffy Monster went to play on Earth with Asp 1932 for a week. They were playing and Fluffy Monster asked to sleep at Asp 1932's house so he did not have to go back home again and again. He said, "Please can I stay for a week?" After a week he went back to Neptune and he had to be alone. No one lived with him. He went all the way back home being really lonely.

Rayhaan Garner (9)
St Silas CE Primary School, Blackburn

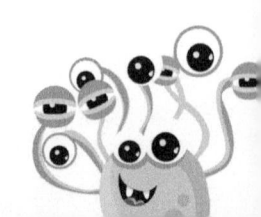

Mrs Sticky Pad

Mrs Sticky Pad is a pad who teleported from place to place and may be good. She went to the bank to see a tornado. She also had an enemy who was called Mr Fluffy. He was good as he wanted to stop the tornado.

One day, Mrs Sticky Pad had an idea. She thought of destroying her enemy's bank. So she requested permission from Mr Fluffy at night to destroy the bank. Even though she did not like her enemy, she knew she had to ask for permission. Only sometimes, she used to meet him as she disliked him.

Arifah Begum (9)
St Silas CE Primary School, Blackburn

Tray Has Stolen

Tray, the red creature, was at school. He desperately needed a pen. The person next to Tray had lots of pens. When he wasn't looking, Tray stole a pen. Navee, who was Tray's sister, saw what Tray had done. After school, Navee explained to Tray that what he had done was wrong. The next day, Tray went to school and apologised to him and brought a new pack of pens just for his friend. His friend was so happy with Tray because he told him the truth. Tray gave a very big hug to Navee.

Layla Shifa (9)
St Silas CE Primary School, Blackburn

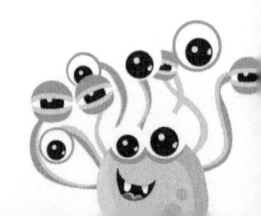

Fluffy Skill

Fluffy Tail had a brother, and they lived in Saturn in space. They had super-speed teleportation and were invincible. His worst enemies were dragons and water. The humans were annoyed at Fluffy Tail and didn't like him. Fluffy Tail went to Earth and made a tsunami to destroy all the buildings. Suddenly his enemy Dragon came and stopped him by going in front of him and distracting him. Everybody saw them. They started to fight, but then Fluffy Tail won and he went to space or Saturn.

Rebin Taher (9)
St Silas CE Primary School, Blackburn

The Great Battle Between Slob Head And Water Magician

The great Slob Head was in his lava house. He came out of his house to meditate, and when he finished meditating, he opened his eyes because he heard something. He looked and saw his enemy, Water Magician, and they had a battle. The battle was great, but in the end, Slob Head threw lava at the Water Magician and hit him. While he threw lava, the Water Magician threw water, but Slob Head won the great, fantastic battle, and the Water Magician wanted his revenge.

Mohammed Khalid (9)
St Silas CE Primary School, Blackburn

Jeff And Billy

Jeff, who was going to rob a bank with his superpowers, went in the night. He planned to use his fire-breathing ability to turn off the cameras and open the safe. Suddenly, Billy attempted to stop him. Jeff used his fire-breathing, causing Billy to become scared and run away. Jeff waited for him. Jeff fire breathed and Billy got marked on his face. Then Billy used his ice powers on Jeff. They both had a fight with their superpowers.

Rayyan Bhayat (9)
St Silas CE Primary School, Blackburn

Mr Moody

One day, there was a big, scary monster called Deathly. He was coming to Earth because humans had attacked him and he wanted revenge. Deathly teleported to a busy place. After that, he shape-shifted into a human, but people still realised he was a monster and they had to hide and defend themselves. They fought back and he injured himself very badly. So he went back to the moon, where he could rest in peace and live by himself.

Sabir Hussain (9)
St Silas CE Primary School, Blackburn

Monster

In Saturn lives ASP 1932, a monster. ASP 1932 has six hands, two legs, eight eyes and fire in his hands to go to different planets.

One day ASP 1932 went to Planet Earth and killed all the people because they thought he was a monster. ASP 1932 is not a very good monster and if you see him, then run away from him very, very, very fast because you'll die from this monster, he is not a good monster.

Albina Nesenenko (9)
St Silas CE Primary School, Blackburn

GangLand Vs Humans

GangLand went to the bank with his gang. They went to the bank for a robbery and put cars around the bank so nobody could go in or out. This way, they could do their job easily and nobody could disturb them. When they were going, people with arms came and said, "Stop right there." Then, GangLand fought them and GangLand won. They went back and then they became rich and they were chilling.

Ibrahim Sher (9)
St Silas CE Primary School, Blackburn

Untitled

Sonic has no friends and goes to a bad home. One day he finds a home where he has friends. In seven days, Doctor Men comes and Sonic fights him. Sonic is so fast and Sonic wins. Sonic then is so happy and goes to help a dog, cat, frog and helps some deer. Doctor Men wants to kill Sonic and Doctor Men is going to kill Sonic and says, "Sorry so much, Sonic." Sonic is happy.

Denis Sercaianu (10)
St Silas CE Primary School, Blackburn

The School's Fire

Humble Hamish liked school and was always happy until one day the school went down! Hamish was up and ready. Hamish sat down and did a couple of maths sums. Hamish's little brother came along.
"Wow, sis, never knew you could do sums that fast," he said in a shocked voice.
"Anyway, gotta go!" she said in a rush. Hamish sat down and sighed.
"Messengers!" the teacher called loudly. Hamish was a messenger, so she ran to the teacher.
"Oh, sorry, Miss," she said, "give this to Miss Mcfarty."
Ring! "Evacuate!" everyone screamed. "There is a fire!"

Fearne Dawson (8)
St Thomas' Primary School, Riddrie

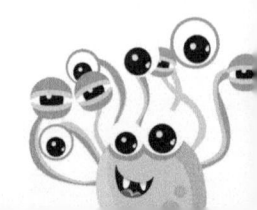

Monster Drama

One scary night there was a monster named Garry. He was a special monster because he was mixed with all the other monsters.
All of the monsters loved him, except for one, Mr Bean. Mr Bean was his enemy. Mr Bean wanted to destroy Monsterland. That was the planet Garry lived on.
"Now I will destroy Monsterland, hahaha!" said Mr Bean. He teleported to Monsterland.
"Oh no!" said Lolo, Lolo was Garry's best friend. Lolo was always worried, but sometimes she wasn't.
All the monsters were angry, especially Garry. They all started fighting and the monsters won.
"Ugh!"
"Yay!"

Myla Donaldson (8)
St Thomas' Primary School, Riddrie

Mr Pickly Pickle

One day, there was a planet called Pickle Planet. A green gooey monster lived on that planet. That monster was called Mr Pickly Pickle. He only ate pickles and goo.

Another monster came to Pickle Planet and that monster was called Catel Monster. He loved Pickle Planet.

Mr Pickly Pickle hated Catel Monster. Catel Monster stole Mr Pickly Pickle's food. He was so angry.

Mr Pickly Pickle tried to kick Catel Monster out. Catel Monster was already leaving.

Mr Pickly Pickle was so happy. "I guess Catel Monster and me are enemies, I'm so happy Catel Monster left my planet."

Dempsey Patterson (8)
St Thomas' Primary School, Riddrie

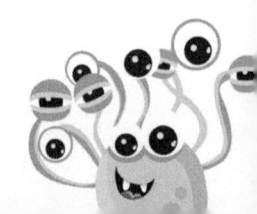

Hero Of Planet Bogie

It was night-time on Planet Bogie. A monster called Pickle Poge was just climbing into bed when the invasion alarm sounded. It was Scary Lery, and he was trying to take over Planet Bogie. Pickle Poge did not like this, and he went to stop him.
Two hours later, he found Scary Lery. "I won't let you do this," said Pickle Poge.
"Try and stop me," said Scary Lery.
Pickle Poge used the power of happiness to blast Scary Lery to the moon.
Pickle Poge woke up. "Wow," he said, "I had the strangest dream. It was so cool."

Charlie Harrigan (8)
St Thomas' Primary School, Riddrie

The Oreo's Adventure

One sunny day there was a bake sale, and in that bake sale, there was an Oreo called Pretty Princess Pink. Then someone picked the Oreo up. The Oreo was scared because she had a friend called Poppy Kind. She didn't want to leave her best friend!
So when the person picked her up and was about to eat her, she opened her eyes. Then the person ran away and told other people.
She told Poppy Kind, "The reason I opened my eyes at the person is because I didn't want to leave you and I wanted to stay here."

Chimamanda Nwankwo (8)
St Thomas' Primary School, Riddrie

The Pink Monster

One sunny day, a creature called Poppy Kind went to school. She was from Pink and Purple Land. Poppy Kind had a bake sale at school. She bought a pink Oreo and she was just about to eat it, and suddenly it opened its eyes. It started to talk. it said her name was Pretty Princess Pink.

The next day they became best friends. They had lunch together and played together. The pink Oreo even had a bed to herself. The next day she took her to school to learn.

At playtime Poppy Kind decided to eat her. Yum yum.

Elyse Bennett (8)
St Thomas' Primary School, Riddrie

The Big Situation At School

Hi, my name is Scary Mary, and I love going to school. Do you know why? Because I like to eat people, jump on them and bite.

When I arrive, everybody jumps on their chairs because they are not excited to see me. When I say hi with my growling voice they are scared and start screaming, and that hurts my ears.

So when I say, "Do you guys have anything I can chew on?" They say no. So I say, "I'll stop eating humans and start eating my enemies... but also humans, sorry."

Uzochi Egbunefu (8)
St Thomas' Primary School, Riddrie

Defeat Pickle Mickle Squgil Jiggle

My monster used a monster rocket to get to Earth to defeat Pickle Mickle Squgil Jiggle. He put a tracker in his bag and he was in Glasgow at St Thomas' trying to steal the secret recipe to make pizza.
Blue Guy got into St Thomas' from a second-floor window because he used a gravel hook and found Pickle Mickle Squgil Jiggle and bit him, and venom juice came out. Then he became so, so famous and he was on the news and newspapers and saved people from all over the world and moon.

Thomas Docherty (7)
St Thomas' Primary School, Riddrie

The Wet Day

One day there was a planet and it was named Eayball Planet, and then something happened. There was a monster. He was walking and he stopped because there was a splash. He looked and he said, "I want to have a splash," then someone came. It was a person. Then the monster said, "I need a home and I don't have money." Then the person said, "I can give you money." The monster said, "Thank you," and that is the finished part.

Chloe Kawalec (7)
St Thomas' Primary School, Riddrie

Griffin The Great

One day there was a little purple monster. His name was Griffin. He was from Planet Glow. He dreamt of being a superhero.

One night, he was dreaming of being a superhero. Suddenly he saw a portal, he entered the portal and he got through the portal. He saw a red monster stuck in a building. He raced up to get her. She was so grateful, she hugged him and said, "Good day."

Then he went through the portal to go home to Planet Glow.

Georgia McConnell (7)
St Thomas' Primary School, Riddrie

The Forbidden Monster Power

Once upon a time, on Mount Everest, there was a war going on with the Blood Hound Men. Their opponents were the Flying Grifon Men.
They were not on Earth, they were on Planet Speckreck. Half of the planet was a Blood Tamia, the other half was Grif Tamia.
The Grifons finished the war by making a catapult and shooting the enemy's base with it.

Nathan Bremner (8)
St Thomas' Primary School, Riddrie

Fluffy

Fluffy died and went to the underworld. He was sad for a while but got used to it. "I'm getting used to this," he said.

He explored the underworld, the devil's room. He was surprised. When he came in, the devil had a big chair, a pitchfork and a scythe. This was a lot of stuff. He felt surprised, shocked and jailed.

Sean-Patrick Miller (8)
St Thomas' Primary School, Riddrie

Mr Stickypads

One day, a man named Mr Stickypads lived on the Planet of Goo. He didn't have any friends. He was lonely. He used to have a best friend, but he was now an enemy called Mr Picky Pickle, plus nobody liked him because he was all gooey.

Grace Fitzpatrick (8)
St Thomas' Primary School, Riddrie

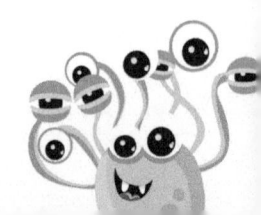

My Crazy Creature

My crazy creature is called Best. Best is an enormous, scary creature with light blue furry skin. He has three eyes and sharp teeth in his belly. He can climb up to the ceiling, then he falls down on people and gobbles them up.

Emmanuel O'Poku (8)
St Thomas' Primary School, Riddrie

YOUNG WRITERS INFORMATION

We hope you have enjoyed reading this book – and that you will continue to in the coming years.

If you're a young writer who enjoys reading and creative writing, or the parent of an enthusiastic poet or story writer, do visit our website **www.youngwriters.co.uk**. Here you will find free competitions, workshops and games, as well as recommended reads, a poetry glossary and our blog.

If you would like to order further copies of this book, or any of our other titles, then please give us a call or visit **www.youngwriters.co.uk**.

Young Writers
Remus House
Coltsfoot Drive
Peterborough
PE2 9BF
(01733) 890066
info@youngwriters.co.uk

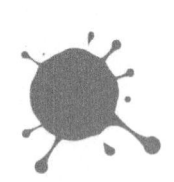

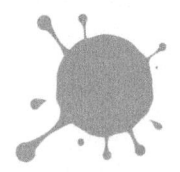

Scan me to watch the Crazy Creatures video!

- YoungWritersUK
- YoungWritersCW
- youngwriterscw
- youngwriterscw